THE SLAUGHTERYARD

Esteban Echeverría

The Slaughteryard

A new translation
by Norman Thomas di Giovanni
and Susan Ashe

Edited, with an Introduction and Notes,
by Norman Thomas di Giovanni

The Friday Project
An imprint of HarperCollins Publishers
77–85 Fulham Palace Road
Hammersmith, London W6 8JB
www.thefridayproject.co.uk
www.harpercollins.co.uk

First published by The Friday Project in 2010

Translation of 'The Slaughteryard' and the Foreword
by Juan María Gutiérrez copyright © 2010
by Norman Thomas di Giovanni and Susan Ashe
Introduction, glossary, and other notes
copyright © 2010 by Norman Thomas di Giovanni
This edition © copyright 2010
by Norman Thomas di Giovanni
www.digiovanni.co.uk

A catalogue record for this book is available
from the British Library

ISBN 978-0-00-734673-8

Designed and typeset by Marcial Souto,
Barcelona and Buenos Aires

Printed in the United States of America

To the memory of Lucilla Muzi,
la garibaldina

CONTENTS

Introduction
Esteban Echeverría and the
Argentine Conscience

I

Years ago, while I worked alongside him in Buenos Aires, Jorge Luis Borges gently urged me to read Argentine authors of the nineteenth century. They were enjoyable and not at all difficult, he told me by way of inducement. And, ever the friend and ambassador of literature, from time to time he presented me with copies of the work of those early writers to which he had contributed his concise, uncomplicated forewords. There were editions of Hilario Ascasubi and Estanislao del Campo, José Hernández and – master of them all – Domingo Faustino Sarmiento. Borges's exhortations eventually proved irresistible. I built myself a small library and at some point took the plunge and acted on his advice.

There are five acknowledged classics of the period in question, cornerstones of Argentine literature and, I would add, of the literature of all Latin America. These are 'El matadero' by

Esteban Echeverría, written in the late 1830s; *Facundo* by Sarmiento, written in 1845; *Amalia* by José Mármol, completed in 1855; *Una escursión a los indios ranqueles* by Lucio Mansilla, written in 1870; and *Martín Fierro* by Hernández, written in 1872 and 1879. The first is a story; the second and fourth extended essays; the third a historical novel; and the last a two-part epic poem of gaucho life.

Borges's encouragement was a gift. Over the years, the leisurely study of these works and of their historical roots in nineteenth-century Argentina has given me considerable pleasure. More, they have helped me draw conclusions about the irrationality of the country, its chronic malaise, its political and economic instability, its capacity – as one historian put it – for self-defeat. The past, indeed, is prologue.

II

'El matadero' – 'The Slaughteryard', as Susan Ashe and I have titled our translation of it – is a work of barely more than thirty pages, but in terms of sheer storytelling and moral authority this handful of pages manages to embrace a considerable range of the concerns of much subsequent Latin-American literature.

Echeverría wrote his story in secret, hidden away at Los Talas, his brother's estancia, or cattle station, some seventy miles distant from Buenos Aires. This was at the height of Juan Manuel de Rosas' reign of terror, which flourished for more than twenty years, from the late 1820s until his downfall in 1852. 'The Slaughteryard', although a work of fiction, is an open indictment of Rosas' ruthless regime. As such, had the tale been discovered, it would have put its author's life in immediate danger. The story's first editor, working from the now lost manuscript, took pains to mention that 'the shakiness ... in the handwriting ... may be the result of rage rather than fear.' While I believe the judgement to be correct, the element of fear cannot be lightly dismissed.

It was not, however, the uncirculated 'Slaughteryard' that ultimately drove Echeverría into Uruguayan exile but, rather, a long series of associations with other young writers and intellectuals, the so-called Generation of 1837. In their uncompromising adherence to the reform and regeneration promised by Argentina's May revolution of 1810, these visionaries became the determined opposition to the despotic Rosas.

But nor did they side with his rivals, whom they regarded as another blood-stained party guilty of sterile factionalism. Echeverría and his group – who were ultimately known as the Association of May – sought, and elaborated in a long series of writings and manifestos, a programme of political and social revolution rooted in democratic ideals. To them, the events of 1810 represented not a simple change of government but the possibility of bringing philosophical thought to bear in the building of a new republican order. The germ of their doctrine was contained in the watchwords *May, Progress, Democracy*.

But there was a more pressing reason for Echeverría's escape abroad. While hiding out at Los Talas, he had set his name to – and probably helped draft – an inflammatory petition that excoriated Rosas, challenged his authority, and supported the much-heralded uprising of 1840. Among the document's eight clauses were these: 'ıst. That Rosas is an abominable tyrant usurper of the sovereignty of the people. 2nd. That Rosas' authority is illegitimate and invalid, and, for this reason, no one is obliged to obey his orders.' As it turned out, the revolt never materialized. The declaration was tantamount to Echeverría's having signed his own death warrant.

In September 1840, he sought safety at first
directly across the River Plate, on the Uruguayan
shore, at Colonia del Sacramento, and ten months
later in Montevideo, where he was to live in
penurious militant exile until his death in 1851.
All his manuscripts had been left behind. 'The
Slaughteryard', never published in its author's
lifetime, was discovered amongst his papers and
printed for the first time in 1871.

III

Esteban Echeverría was born in 1805 to a well-off
Buenos Aires family. The second of nine children,
he grew up in the very neighbourhood on the
city's south side where his tale takes place. Five
years later came the May revolution, the earth-
shaking event that severed the Viceroyalty of
the Río de la Plata from the Spanish Crown and
plunged a set of bitterly disunited provinces into
decades of turmoil, chaos, and bloody civil war.
For Echeverría it was also the event that became
the focus of his intellectual life. His father died
in 1816; his mother, in 1822. By this time he had
begun a course of preparatory studies in Latin
and philosophy at the fledgling University of

Buenos Aires, which he relinquished after two years to take up employment as an apprentice clerk in an import–export firm. Here, on his own, he perfected French. At the age of twenty, restless and dissatisfied with the poor prospects for study in his own country, Echeverría looked to Europe to satisfy his thirst for knowledge and so, in the autumn of 1825 – with the blessing of his employers – he set sail for France.

In Paris over the next four years Echeverría studied haphazardly at various institutions, delving into mathematics, geography, political economy, law; he was also tutored in the guitar and drawing. With recommendations from his Buenos Aires employer, many doors were opened to him, and he sat in on lectures by distinguished professors and attended salons, where he met celebrities such as Benjamin Constant, the enemy of despotism and staunch partisan of the rule of law. At the same time Echeverría read and read with a voracious appetite. In social theory: Montesquieu, Sismondi, Lerminier, Lammenais, Guizot, Vico, Saint-Marc Girardin, Vinet, Chateaubriand, Pascal. In literature: Shakespeare, Schiller, Goethe, Byron, Hugo. The new political theory of liberalism inspired him, as did the new literary concept of romanticism. Romanticism, said

Echeverría, repeating Victor Hugo, was liberalism in literature. He began writing poetry. And then, prior to returning home, he spent a month and a half in London.

When Echeverría at last disembarked in the roadstead off Buenos Aires in late June 1830, Rosas had been in power for seven months. The city had changed. The tyrant had set in motion the tireless persecution of his enemies, and the old climate of freedom was over. Those who opposed Rosas were obliged either to seek refuge abroad or simply to go to ground.

'The country no longer existed,' Echeverría was to record. And yet, despite his withdrawn, melancholic nature, he remained essentially undaunted. Within a fortnight, two of his poems appeared – unsigned – in a Buenos Aires newspaper, and the young poet was at work on his first book. The legacy of his European learning, meanwhile, gradually fermented. Slowly Echeverría found himself, and even more slowly he emerged and mixed with young men of his own age and outlook. Thus, invisibly, almost without premeditation, the seed of resistance to Rosas became implanted. Seven years passed. In this span, Echeverría published two widely acclaimed volumes of poetry – *Los consuelos*, in 1834, and

Rimas, in 1837. The seed of opposition now began to sprout.

The two titles are today enshrined in Latin-American literary history. With *Los consuelos* Echeverría introduced romanticism not only to the River Plate but also to all of Latin America and even to Spain. This was part and parcel of the author's programme of regeneration, for previously all new intellectual and artistic currents had come from Madrid. With *Rimas* and its 2,100-line centrepiece, 'La cautiva', Echeverría achieved another first. The poem, using the pampa as its setting, was the earliest instance in Latin America of a local landscape serving as a theme of literary inspiration. This set a precedent throughout the Spanish-speaking New World. Echeverría was now looked on by his peers as their natural leader and as such he was pressed to the fore.

IV

The period, a dramatic highpoint of Argentine history, is richly documented. The young men of the 1837 generation were educated, literate, articulate; their sudden proscription and dispersal abroad created a wide network, an underground activism. The ensuing correspondence among them was voluminous, as were their writings, which were printed, reprinted, and circulated in a wide range of opposition newspapers in Montevideo and Valparaíso and Santiago de Chile and Paris, as well as in a number of cities of the Argentine interior.

Fittingly, the movement began in the back room of a bookshop and lending library – Marcos Sastre's Librería Argentina. Two years earlier, in 1835, the government had begun closing down teaching posts at the university and the students, to their dismay, were obliged to pledge themselves to 'the national cause of Federalism', Rosas' faction. The ensuing unrest and the general climate of growing repression coincided with the launch of the Literary Salon founded by Sastre in his shop, in June 1837. As Juan María Gutiérrez, Echeverría's biographer, recorded, 'a secret mutual attraction' grew up between the disaffected students and the Salon, which was 'a kind of institution or free academy where friends of literature gathered to read, debate, and converse'. Here Echeverría read sections from his poem 'La cautiva' and found himself in the midst of an audience of youthful intelligentsia who were passionate about aesthetics and about freedom.

But political discussion was off limits, and within six months Rosas had banned the Salon's activities, obliging Sastre to sell off his books at auction.

The work of the movement, renamed the Asociación de la Joven Generación Argentina, now became secret and their meetings clandestine. One night, in June 1838, as Echeverría was later to chronicle (*Ojeada retrospectiva*, II):

... almost spontaneously, some thirty or thirty-five young men came together in a spacious locality, their faces displaying restless curiosity and joyous affection. The undersigned, after sketching the moral predicament of Argentine youth, ... pointed out the importance of their joining together so as to know one another and to be strong, fraternizing in both thought and action. He then read the *symbolic words* that crown our beliefs. An electric explosion of enthusiasm and joy greeted these words of brotherhood and solidarity; they were, it seemed, the eloquent revelation of a thought shared by all, and they summed up emblematically the desires and hopes of indissoluble comradeship.

Now, after so many disappointments and struggles, we take pleasure in recalling that most beautiful night in our life, for neither before nor after have we felt such deep, pure feelings of patriotism.

The meetings of this secret society nurtured the germ of what became – to give it its full title – the *Dogma socialista de la asociación Mayo*. First published anonymously in parts and under various titles in Uruguayan periodicals at the end of 1838 and early in 1839, the work was ultimately revised and enlarged for its appearance in book form, in Montevideo, in 1846. Its title today, usually shortened to two words, strikes an unfortunate note. By *dogma* Echeverría meant simply 'creed' or 'beliefs' and by *socialista* he meant 'social'. Social Creed or Social Credo or the Social Contract was the intended meaning. The essay, written in concentrated, lucid, impeccable prose, presents a plan for the future organization of the country. It begins with a backward glance at the Association's early history – the aforementioned *Ojeada retrospectiva sobre el movimiento intelectual en el Plata desde el año 37* – and then goes on to outline the movement's central tenets in an elaboration of fourteen key words. The style is pithy and aphoristic ('Egoism is the death of the soul'; 'All privilege is a crime against equality'), with overtones of the beatitudes and of the Bible in general.

Within months of its publication, *Dogma socialista* was reviewed at considerable length in the columns of the *Archivo americano*, an official organ of the Rosas regime. The author of the notice, who claimed the book a 'libel', was the paper's editor, Pedro de Angelis. At one point de Angelis writes:

If he [Echeverría] were able to get out of his revolutionary paroxism, he would then perceive how extravagant the idea was of regenerating a people by means of a few young men, without credit, without connexions, without resources, who 'some viewed with distrust, and others with contempt:' he would comprehend all the ridiculousness of wishing to convert the Argentines into a society of *St. Simonians*, of submitting a Republic, founded upon the general principles of the modern organization of states, to the delirium of Fourier and Considerant. In this alone he has given us the proof of the complete aberration of his mind …

(The *Archivo* was printed in three parallel columns of Spanish, French, and English; the above is cited from the paper's own often idiosyncratic English.)

The review unleashed an immediate response, a measured attack in the form of two extensive open letters that were later published together as a pamphlet of fifty-nine pages. Wading straight in, Echeverría thanks de Angelis for his 'present':

Your gift does not surprise me; it is the only thing you and your co-authors can offer. In it, as in everything else, the conduct of the heroic founder of the *American System* [Rosas] follows a logic: those who are not with him but are near at hand, he decapitates; those who have put themselves outside his reach, he slanders and defames through the mouth of his lackeys. It is undeniable that you fill the office to perfection.

Echeverría obviously revelled in the seemingly effortless stream of invective that flowed from his pen. He was, as so much of his writing reveals – and nowhere more than in these epistles – a consummate polemicist. As models of the genre and a useful adjunct to *Dogma socialista*, they can still be read and studied with pleasure.

The Argentine critic and literary historian Ricardo Rojas noted that in the pages of *Dogma socialista* 'breathes the lofty spirit that led a whole generation to the noble sacrifice of exiling itself from an unworthy native land or remaining there to die in the name of freedom.' Rojas judged Echeverría's book to be 'one of the ten or twenty works that every Argentine must read'.

But such a massive flight had other consequences. The homeland became a desert of ideas, so much so that in 1849 a French traveller observed, 'I can say in all sincerity that literature does not exist in Buenos Aires.'

V

'The Slaughteryard' is reputed to be the most widely studied school text in all Spanish America. It's easy to see how a story that is vividly told and that touches on still unsettled questions of oppression and repression, poverty and corruption – and that, moreover, features an untarnished hero in confrontation with mob violence – strikes a responsive chord with readers. The tale's continued popularity underlines the universality of moral issues.

In 'The Slaughteryard' and in *Dogma socialista* – as well as in a series of long poems – Echeverría's aim, his programme, matches that of James Joyce, who sought to forge in the smithy of his soul the uncreated conscience of his race. That Echeverría's ambitious endeavour, the complete reformation of Argentine society, stalled with his death was neither the fault of his vision nor of his impassioned reasoning. For a myriad of reasons, the raw, unformed nation proved incapable of renouncing the values of violence and regressive barbarism. What followed was the perpetuation of an exclusive society based on the narrow interests of landed wealth rather than the creation of an open society rooted in social justice. Ever since, Argentines have thrashed and lurched about in the snares of authoritarianism and militarism, those twin catastrophes of any system of government. This course reached its culmination in the infamous Dirty War of the 1970s and the intemperate invasion of the Falkland Islands in the 1980s – events that have morally bankrupted the Argentine nation and ravaged the psyche of its people.

Echeverría's life and his heroic labours were consecrated to high-minded ideals. An intellectual warrior, he literally worked himself into his grave for the betterment of his native land, to which he was never able to return. He died at the age of forty-five, twelve or so months before the collapse of the Rosas tyranny, an event he was robbed of witnessing and savouring.

In 1871, Echeverría's friend and editor Juan María Gutiérrez wrote in his foreword to the first publication of 'The Slaughteryard':

A country that, for whatever reason, appears indifferent to its history and allows much of it to drift into oblivion is doomed to remain without a face of its own and to seem to the world insipid and bloodless. And if this failure to fulfil an obligation is the deliberate result of misconceived patriotism, which silences mistakes and crimes, then the omission is all the more deplorable. To serve a country's honour in such a way is no virtue but a crime dearly paid for, since it renders history useless either as an example or as a basis for reform.

History drifting into oblivion. A sad epitaph but a true indictment of Argentina's divided society and its unending support of demagoguery and despotism.

Today Echeverría is honoured by a township on the southern edge of Buenos Aires that bears his name; he is also commemorated in bronze in the heart of the city itself, at the meeting of Florida and Santa Fe. On the plinth of this impressive statue are carved a handful of his uncompromising maxims: *Miserables de aquellos que vacilan cuando la tiranía se ceba en las entrañas de la patria* – 'Wretched are those who falter when tyranny feeds on the entrails of the nation.' Alas, such words express sentiments that Argentines have seldom been able to live up to.

The greatest portion of what Echeverría wrote

is now neglected, but nonetheless his pages stand – an uncomfortable and inconvenient reminder of the truth.

Norman Thomas di Giovanni
Keyhaven, Lymington
Hampshire
November 2009

Note to the Reader

It may prove useful before beginning Echeverría's story to dip into the headnote on p. 35 and then to peruse the Glossary.

THE SLAUGHTERYARD

Despite the fact that I am writing history, I shall not copy the early Spanish chroniclers of America, who are held up to us as models, and go back to Noah's ark and the generations of his family. There are plenty of reasons for ignoring such an example, but to avoid long-windedness I shall pass over them and say only that the events of my story took place at the end of the 1830s. It was during Lent, a period when in Buenos Aires meat is in short supply, since the Church – adopting Epictetus's dictum, *sustine, abstine* – ordains fasting and abstinence for the stomachs of the faithful on the grounds that the flesh is sinful and, according to the proverb, flesh seeks flesh. And since from the beginning the Church, by God's direct command, has held spiritual sway over both consciences and stomachs – which in no way belong to the individual – nothing is more just or reasonable than that the Church should forbid wrongdoing.

The victuallers, knowing as good Federalists

and therefore good Catholics that the people of Buenos Aires are peculiarly inclined to obey orders of any sort, during Lent take to the slaughteryard only enough young steers to feed the children and the sick, as is allowed by papal bull. It is no part of the victuallers' intention to sate a handful of monstrous heretics, who are always about, ready to break the Church's butcherous laws and contaminate society by setting a bad example.

At the time in question, there had been a lot of rain. Roads were awash, the marshes lay under water, and every street leading into the city oozed a runny mud. In a sudden mighty rush, the Riachuelo burst its banks, until its thickly silted waters spread majestically to the foot of the San Pedro bluffs. The swollen River Plate repelled the waters that were trying to flow into it, inundating fields, dikes, copses, farmsteads, and turned all low-lying ground into an immense lake. Girdled from north to east by water and mud, and to the south by a whitish sea over whose surface a handful of little boats bobbed aimlessly and chimney stacks and treetops loomed black, the towers and heights of the city cast a baffled look to the horizon, as if begging the Almighty for mercy. A new Flood seemed at hand. Devout men and women whimpered novenas and an unending stream of prayers. Preachers thundered in the temples and made the pulpits groan with the hammering of their fists. Judgement Day is at hand, they cried, the end of the world is nigh. God's wrath has been roused and is spilling over. Woe unto you, ye sinners! Woe unto you, ye godless Unitarians, who mock the Church and her saints and listen not with veneration to the word of the Lord's anointed! Woe unto you unless you throw yourselves at the foot of the altar and plead for mercy! The awful hour of vain gnashing of teeth and frenzied supplication approaches. Your wickedness, your heresy, your blasphemies, your horrendous crimes, have brought God's plagues upon us. The God of the Federation in His justice will pronounce you damned.

Women staggered from the temple, distraught, blaming the Unitarians – as was only to be expected – for the calamity that had befallen them.

Still the torrential rains came down, and the flood waters rose, fulfilling the prophecies of the preachers. On the order of the Most Catholic Restorer, the bells began to toll for prayers, though not all of them, it seems, were ranged on his side. The libertines, the unbelievers – the Unitarians, that is – were soon intimidated by the sight of all the contrite faces and by the din of the curses heaped on them. As if it had already been decided on, everyone was talking about a procession in which the whole city would march bareheaded and unshod, accompanying the Host, borne by the bishop under a canopy, to the steep banks at Balcarce, where thousands of voices, exorcizing the Unitarian devil of the flood waters, would cry aloud for God's divine mercy.

Luckily – or unfortunately, rather, because the event would have been something to behold – the ceremony did not take place, for the River Plate fell, and its waters gradually subsided back into its immense course without need either of exorcism or prayer.

The point of all this is that, owing to the flood, for a whole fortnight the Convalecencia, or Alto, slaughteryard saw not a single head of cattle, while in only a day or two all the oxen belonging to smallholders and water-carriers were used up in provisioning the city. The sick and the children of the poor ate eggs and chickens, while foreigners and heretics bellowed for steak and roasts. Abstinence from meat was widespread amongst the people, who had never before made themselves so worthy of the Church's blessing, and thus it was that plenary indulgences rained down on them by the million. The price of poultry shot up to six pesos, eggs to four reales, and fish became extremely dear. During that Lent there was no eating of meat and fish at the same meal, nor were there excesses of gluttony. Instead, countless souls went straight to heaven, and things took place that now seem unreal.

Of the many thousands of rats that made their home in the slaughteryard, not one remained alive. They all starved to death or were drowned in their holes by the relentless rain. A horde of black women, out scavenging offal like buzzards, prowled the city like so many Harpies, ready to devour whatever edible matter they found. Their inseparable rivals in the shambles, dogs and gulls, ranged far afield in search of carrion. A number of the sick wasted away from lack of hot food; but the most remarkable occurrence was the almost instant death of a large number of foreign heretics who committed the sacrilege of gorging on Extremadura sausages, ham, and cod, for which they were dispatched to the other world to pay for the abominable sin of mixing meat and fish.

Some physicians were of the opinion that, if meat privation went on, half the population would collapse, since their stomachs were accustomed to its fortifying juices. This gloomy scientific prognosis appeared to fly in the face of the denunciations hurled from the pulpit on all forms of animal sustenence and on eating meat and fish during days set aside for fast and penitence. A kind of intestinal struggle between stomachs and consciences arose, triggered by relentless appetites and by the no less relentless rantings of the clergy, who, mindful of their duty, gave no quarter to any vice that involved the relaxing of Catholic customs. As a result of the diet of fish and beans and other somewhat indigestible foods, everyone suffered the additional affliction of flatulence.

This struggle manifested itself in unrestrained sobbing and groaning during the climax of the sermons and in sudden rumblings and explosions in the houses and streets of the city or anywhere else that people congregated. Ever paternalistic and provident, the Restorer's government grew alarmed. Believing the uproar to be of revolutionary origin and attributing it to the barbarous Unitarians, whose wickedness – according to the Federalist preachers – had brought the flood of divine wrath down on the country, the government took preventive measures. They sent spies amongst the people, and, having assessed the resulting reports, in order to quieten both consciences and stomachs they brought in a law with the wise and pious preamble that, by hook or by crook – flood waters notwithstanding – cattle should be brought to the stockyards.

Accordingly, on the sixteenth day of the dearth, which happened to fall on the eve of Our Lady of the Sorrows, a herd of fifty fat bullocks swam the Riachuelo at the ferry crossing and made their way to the Alto slaughteryard. For a city used to a daily consumption of two hundred and fifty to three hundred head, this was not a great number, especially since a good third of the population would be enjoying a dispensation from the Lenten ban on eating meat. How odd that some stomachs should be privileged and some bound by inviolable laws, and that the Church should hold the key to both!

But maybe it is not odd, since it is by way of the flesh that the devil most often finds his way into the body, while it is the Church that has the power to cast him out. The consequence is that man is reduced to a machine whose mainspring is not his own free will but the will of the Church and the government. Perhaps the day is not far off when to breathe the free air, to stroll about, and even to chat to a friend will be forbidden without the consent of the requisite authority. This is more or less how it was in the happier days of our sainted forefathers, which, unfortunately, the May revolution threw into disarray.

Whatever the case, at the news of the government's forethought – and in spite of mud, slaughterers, offal butchers, and waiting onlookers, who welcomed the fifty bullocks with much rejoicing and applause – the stockyard pens began to fill.

'Small but fat,' the people cried. 'Three cheers for the Federation! Hurrah for the Restorer!'

The reader should understand that in those days the Federation was always at hand, even in the filth of the slaughteryard, and, just as there is no sermon without mention of St Augustine, there was no festivity where the Restorer was not in evidence. On hearing the tumultuous roar – so the story goes – every last rat starving in its hole revived and scampered about, assured that, heralded by the sound of joy and revelry, abundance was returning to its customary place.

The whole carcass of the first animal to be slaughtered was presented to the Restorer, who was very partial to roast meat. A delegation of butchers marched off to deliver it in the name of the stockyard's Federalists. In this way, they showed in person their gratitude for the government's fitting gesture, as well as their boundless devotion to the Restorer and their deep-seated hatred of the barbarous Unitarians, those enemies of both God and man. The Restorer replied to the speech in like manner, and the ceremony ended with a due chorus of cheers and hurrahs from the spectators and the participants. It is thought that the Restorer had special permission from His Eminence not to abstain from meat, for, otherwise, as a close observer of the laws, a good Catholic, and a staunch defender of the faith, he would never have set the bad example of accepting such a gift on a holy day.

The slaughter began, and within a quarter of an hour forty-nine steers were hanging in the open yard, some flayed and others about to be. Although it represented all that was ugly, dirty, and hideous about a small proletarian class peculiar to the River Plate, the spectacle was lively and colourful. Perhaps a brief sketch of the venue will help the reader to take in the scene at a glance.

The Alto slaughteryard is a big open area, rectangular in shape, set among small farms on the city's south side. Two roads lead to the place, one of them stopping there and the other continuing east. The ground, which falls away southward, is bisected by a ditch, carved by rainwater, whose banks are riddled with rat holes and whose bed, when it pours, collects all the slaughteryard's fresh or dried blood. In one corner on the west side stands the counting-house, a low, three-roomed wooden construction, with a veranda in front facing the road and a rail for tethering horses. Behind the building are a number of stockades made out of *ñandubay* posts, with sturdy gates for shutting in the cattle.

In winter, these pens are a positive morass, in which the overcrowded animals sink up to their withers and remain stuck fast, almost unable to move. The counting-house contains an office for collecting taxes on the livestock. Here too fines are imposed by the slaughteryard judge, an important figure, the chief of the butchers, who – by the authority of the Restorer – wields supreme power in that small republic. It is easy to imagine the sort of man required to carry out such a task. The structure, moreover, is so small and so dilapidated that it would escape notice if the formidable judge were not associated with it and if the following legends did not stand out in red letters on its white front: 'The Federation Forever', 'Long Live the Restorer and Our Heroine doña Encarnación Ezcurra', 'Death to the Barbarous Unitarians'. Inscriptions of great significance, reflecting the political and religious faith of the personnel of the slaughteryard. Some readers, however, may not know that the aforementioned heroine was the Restorer's late wife, beloved patroness of the butchers, and that although she was dead they still worshipped her for her Christian virtues and her Federalist heroism during the uprising against Balcarce. The story goes that on one anniversary of that memorable achievement by the Mazorca, the butchers entertained their heroine in the counting-house with a splendid banquet, an event she attended with her daughter and other Federalist ladies, and where, before a large gathering, she pledged with a solemn toast her Federalist patronage to the gentlemen butchers. For this they enthusiastically proclaimed her patroness of the slaughteryard and inscribed her name on the outside walls in letters that will remain in place until erased by the hand of time.

Seen from afar, the slaughteryard appeared to hum with grotesque activity. Forty-nine steers hung there, and some two hundred people trampled over that muddy stretch of ground, which was watered by blood from the beasts' arteries. Each carcass was ringed by a group of human figures of varying race and colour. Prominent in every group was a butcher, a knife in his hand, forearms and chest bared, his long hair matted, his shirt, *chiripá*, and face smeared with blood. Behind him, twisting and turning to follow his every move, was a milling entourage of louts and black and mulatto scavengers – women as ugly as Harpies – amongst whom mastiffs sniffed and growled, nipping at each other over their quarry. Forty-odd ox carts covered with tanned and blackened hides waited in an untidy row the whole length of the open ground, while horsemen in ponchos, their coiled lassos hitched to their saddles, threaded their way along the line towards the gate or, leaning on the necks of their mounts, cast a lazy eye over one or another of the squabbling groups. At the same time, overhead, a flock of glinting white gulls, lured off their course by the smell of flesh, wheeled and, with their squawks, drowned out the uproar of the slaughteryard as they cast a bright shadow on that field of carnage. Such was the scene when the slaughtering began.

But on closer inspection, the view changed. The little gatherings broke up, sometimes to re-form, sometimes to scatter as if a stray bullet or raging dog had plunged among them. In one group a butcher quartered a carcass with an axe, in another he hung the pieces on hooks in his cart, in still another he flayed off a hide, and in a fourth he trimmed away the tallow. Meanwhile from out of the mob, which kept a close eye on its quarry of offal, a grimy hand reached out now and again to hack at the tallow or at the meat, causing the butcher to howl in rage, the jostling groups to seethe, and the youths to bawl out a torrent of oaths.

'That hag's tucked some tallow between her tits,' cried one.

'He shoved a chunk down his fly,' the black woman retorted.

'Hey you, black witch, be off or I'll carve you up,' called out the butcher.

'Come on, master, don't be stingy. All I want is the belly and guts.'

'They're for that witch over there, so piss off now.'

'The witch! The witch!' chimed the youths. 'She's taking the kidney fat and the gullet.' And gobbets of blood and huge clods of mud rained down on the woman's head.

Elsewhere, two African women were dragging off a heap of entrails. Clutching an armload of intestines, a mulatto crone slipped in a puddle of blood and fell headlong onto her ill-gotten booty. Four hundred black women squatted in rows, unravelling strings of guts on their skirts and picking out one by one the few lumps of tallow that a butcher's miserly knife had left behind like stragglers. Others emptied stomachs and bladders and inflated them so that once dry they could be used to carry the offal.

A number of urchins dodged about on foot or on horseback, swiping at each other with bladders and hurling chunks of meat about. The missiles and the commotion scattered the cloud of gulls that hovered overhead, shrieking in celebration of the slaughter. Despite the Restorer's decree and the holiness of the day, obscene and filthy words – redolent of the beastly cynicism that characterizes the rabble of Buenos Aires slaughteryards – arose from every quarter, but I shall not regale the reader with them.

All at once a blood-soaked lung fell on a man's head, and he crowned someone else with it, at which point a hideous mastiff snatched it up in mid-air and a pack of dogs – which may or may not have had a chance of getting any of the spoil – set up a frightful snarling and snapping. An old woman shot off in furious pursuit of an urchin who had daubed her face with blood. Flocking to their shouts and swearing, his fellow thieves surrounded and baited her as if they were dogs around a bull, pelting her with bits of meat and dung, and guffawing and bellowing. To restore order, the judge cleared the ground.

Two boys then began to show off their skill at knife play, violently slashing and thrusting at each other; nearby, four older lads, also armed with knives, disputed the ownership of a large intestine and a tripe they had stolen from one of the butchers; and a few yards away some dogs, scrawny from their involuntary fast, also scrapped to settle which of them would carry off a liver covered in mud. All this was a reflection in miniature of the savage manner in which individuals and society claim their rights and thrash out their disputes in our country. In short, the events taking place in the slaughteryard had to be seen to be believed.

One fierce-looking animal was still in the pen. It had a thick neck, and from its genitals opinions differed as to whether it was a bull or a bullock. The creature's time had come. Two mounted lassoers forced a way into the corral, round which the mob swarmed, some on foot, some on horseback, with others sitting astride the rough posts. In the gateway stood a strange and striking group of men, sleeves rolled up, armed with trusty lassos for roping a steer's legs. Each wore a head scarf, waistcoat, and *chiripá* in Federalist scarlet. Behind them, a number of riders and other spectators watched with an eager, critical eye.

The animal, now roped by the horns, bellowed

and foamed at the mouth in fury, and not even the devil himself could have driven the beast out of the clinging mud in which it was stuck fast. To rope its legs was impossible. From their perch on the corral posts, the louts taunted the animal, trying to provoke it with their ponchos and neckerchiefs. The deafening hullabaloo unleashed by that bizarre orchestra – a torrent of catcalls, clapping, and shouts from bass and treble voices – was something to hear.

Wisecracks and obscenities passed from mouth to mouth, and, fired up by the spectacle or by someone else's caustic tongue, each man or boy made a show of his own wit.

'Fucking bull.'

'Fuck all gelded bulls from Azul.'

'Bloody drover, giving us cat and pretending it's hare.'

'Hare? It's a bullock.'

'An old bull, you mean.'

'What bull? Show me its balls, asshole!'

'There they are, between its legs. Can't you see them, pal? They're bigger than your horse's head – or did you go blind on the way here?'

'Your mother went blind – the day she laid eyes on you. Can't you see what's hanging there is mud?'

'You're as pigheaded as a Unitarian.'

At this magic word, the whole crowd roared out, 'Death to the barbarous Unitarians!'

'And to One Eye, a pair of balls.'

'Yes, the balls to take on the Unitarians.'

'And to butcher Matasiete, throat-slitter to the Unitarians, the best joint. Three cheers for Matasiete!'

'The best joint for Matasiete!'

'The bull's off!' shouted a gruff voice, cutting through the cowardly jeers. 'There it goes!'

'Careful! Look out, you lot by the gate. He's a vicious devil!'

The animal, tormented by the clamour and even more by the two sharp prods that jabbed its rump – and at the same time sensing a slackness in the lasso – charged the gate, casting a baleful look around out of blazing, reddish eyes. On his horse, the man with the lasso pulled hard at the bullock, the rope jerked free of the animal's horns and hissed through the air. From the corral fencepost, a boy's head – severed as if by an axe blow – rolled into the pen, while the torso remained in place on its wooden horse, a long spurt of blood jetting out of each artery.

'The rope's taken off his head,' someone shouted.

'There goes the bull,' yelled someone else, while

the rest were struck dumb by the suddenness of what had happened.

The group at the gate split into two. Horrified, half rushed towards the boy's head and throbbing corpse, while the remainder, who had not witnessed the accident, rode off in different directions in pursuit of the animal.

'After it!' they bellowed. 'Watch out there! Head it off!'

'Use your rope, Sietepelos.'

'Careful you aren't gored, lad!'

'It's gone mad. Everyone out of its way.'

'Head it off, head it off, you coward!'

'Give your nag a taste of spurs.'

'The bull's out in the road.'

'There's nothing for it, then!'

The tumult increased. Hearing it, the row of black women who were still scavenging offal beside the ditch threw themselves down onto the stomachs and intestines that they had been unravelling with the patience of a Penelope. The action probably saved them, for as soon as the animal set eyes on the women it let out a hideous bellow, leapt aside, and, pursued by the horsemen, plunged on. The story goes that one of the women emptied her bowels, that another said ten Hail Marys in a minute or so, and that two more swore to San Benito that they would give up scavenging for good and never again set foot in that damned stockyard. No one knows whether they kept their vows.

The bull, meanwhile, lit off for the city down a long, narrow street that led from one corner of the rectangle described above. This street, known as Only Street because it only had a couple of houses on it, was flanked on either side by a ditch and a cactus hedge. The whole middle of the road was a deep mire that stretched from ditch to ditch. A certain Englishman, returning from his meat-salting factory, was just then picking his way through the morass on a somewhat skittish horse. Absorbed in his calculations, he heard neither the oncoming horsemen nor the shouting until the moment the bull came hurtling into the boggy stretch of ground. Startled, the Englishman's horse reared and bucked and broke into a gallop, leaving the unfortunate man floundering in two feet of mud. This incident, however, did not halt or even slow down the bull's pursuers, who, in fact, hooted with sarcastic laughter.

'The gringo's out of sorts,' they mocked. 'Get up, gringo.' And they trampled his wretched body in the mud under the hooves of their horses.

As best he could, the Englishman struggled to

the edge of the mire, looking more like a devil blackened by the flames of hell than a white man with blond hair.

Farther down the road, at a cry of 'The bull! Look out for the bull!', four black scavengers on their way home with their plunder took refuge in the only available spot – the water-filled ditch.

The animal, meanwhile, having covered a good mile and a half – running first one way, then the other – and terrifying every living thing with its presence, entered the gate of a small farmstead, where it met its doom. Although tired, it showed its mettle in an angry scowl, but it was hemmed in by a deep ditch and a thick hedge of prickly pear, with no way out. The bull's pursuers, who had split up, now rejoined forces and decided to lure the animal back with tame oxen so that it could expiate its crime in the place where the offence had been committed.

An hour after its flight, the bull was once more in the slaughteryard, where what remained of the crowd could talk of nothing but the beast's trangressions. The episode of the gringo in the mud provoked only laughter and derision. All that was left of the boy beheaded by the lasso was a puddle of blood. His body was in the cemetery.

The animal, now rearing and snorting and

pawing the ground, was soon roped by the horns. One after another, three attempts were made to snare its legs, but to no avail. A fourth throw caught one hoof. The bull's vigour and rage redoubled; its panting tongue spewed foam; its nostrils, steam; its eyes, fire.

'Hamstring it!' called out a peremptory voice.

Matasiete leapt off his horse and with a single stroke slashed the bull's tendon. Next, dodging round the animal with his enormous knife in hand, he sank it to the hilt in the beast's throat, then held the steaming red blade up to the onlookers. Blood gushing from its wound, the splendid creature let out a few hoarse bellows, faltered, and collapsed to the cheers of the mob, who proclaimed Matasiete victor and awarded him the choicest joint. Once more Matasiete proudly threw up his arm and blood-stained knife, and then he and his fellow butchers squatted down to flay the hide.

There still remained the question of the genitalia of the dead beast, whose stubborn ferocity had provisionally caused it to be classified as a bull, but everyone was so worn out by the long chase that for the time being they forgot about the matter. Then all at once a gruff voice called out, 'Here are its balls!', and one of the butchers drew from under the animal's belly and held up to the crowd two enormous testicles – unmistakable proof of the animal's dignified status. Guffaws and loud talk erupted; all the mishaps were now easily explained. A bull in the slaughteryard was a rare, not to say forbidden, event. Such a creature, according to the rules, should have been thrown to the dogs, but meat was so scarce and so many people were hungry that the judge had simply turned a blind eye.

In no time at all the much-reviled bull was skinned, cut into joints, and hanging in a cart. Matasiete tucked his prize joint under the sheep-skin that served as his saddle and got ready to leave. The slaughter was over by twelve o'clock, and the small throng that had stayed to the very end left in twos and threes on foot, on horseback, or driving the last of the carts loaded with meat.

Just then the guttural voice of one of the butchers shouted, 'Here comes a Unitarian!'

Hearing the inflammatory word, the entire mob stopped in its tracks.

'Look at his U-shaped beard. And he's not wearing a red ribbon on his tail-coat or a mourning band on his hat.'

'Unitarian dog.'

'See his fancy city clothes.'

'And he's using an English saddle.'

'Give him a taste of the corn-cob.'

'Or a shearing.'

'He needs taking down a peg.'

'Showing off with those holsters.'

'All these fancy-arse Unitarians are show-offs.'

'Are you up to it, then, Matasiete?'

'Well, are you or not?'

'I say he is.'

Matasiete was a man of few words and much action. When it came to violence, agility, skill with an axe, knife, or horse, he said nothing but simply acted. Now he had been provoked. Spurring his mount, he loosened his reins and rode straight for the Unitarian.

The young man, who was about twenty-five, spruce and well-turned out, had been riding to Barracas without the slightest fear of danger when the torrent of jibes spewed from those uncouth mouths. Seeing the ominous looks of that pack of slaughteryard dogs, the newcomer automatically reached a hand for the holsters on his English saddle, but a sideways shove by Matasiete's horse knocked him over the hindquarters of his mount, throwing him flat on his back, where he lay still.

'Hurrah for Matasiete!' shouted the mob, flocking to close in on the victim like birds of prey on the skeleton of an ox slain by a jaguar.

Still dazed, and casting a furious glance at the brutes around him, the young man made for his horse, which stood a few yards off, to seek redress and vengeance with his pistols. Springing to the ground, Matasiete waylaid him, seized him by the cravat with one hefty arm and threw him down. Drawing his knife from his belt, the butcher held it to the other's throat.

A hoot of laughter and a new rousing cheer once more hailed Matasiete.

What nobility of soul! What courage the Federalists had! Always in a gang, falling like vultures on a helpless victim.

'Cut his throat, Matasiete. He was going for his pistols. Slit his throat the way you slit the bull's.'

'Two-faced Unitarian. He needs shearing.'

'He has a fine throat for the violin.'

'Play the violin on his throat.'

'Make him dance in his own blood.'

'Let's have a try,' said Matasiete, leering. Pinning the young man's chest with his left knee and gripping him by the hair, the butcher drew the edge of his knife across the fallen victim's throat.

'No, don't cut his throat,' came the commanding voice of the slaughteryard judge as he rode up.

'To the counting-house!'

'Take him to the counting-house.'

'Get the corn-cob and shears ready.'

'Death to the barbarous Unitarians!'

'Three cheers for the Restorer of the Laws!'

'Three cheers for Matasiete!'

Again the chorus of spectators roared approval and shouted for death. Binding the unfortunate young man's arms behind him, with blows and shoves, jeers and insults, they dragged him to the torture bench just as His tormentors did to Christ.

In the middle of the room stood a big heavy table that was never clear of glasses and playing cards except when they were removed to make way for torture or an execution by the slaughteryard's Federalist killers. In one corner stood another smaller table, laid out with writing materials and a notebook and surrounded by a few chairs, prominent among them that of the judge. One man, by appearance a soldier, sat there accompanying himself on a guitar as he sang a song highly popular amongst the Federalists about dancing in the slippery blood of a slit throat, when the throng of rabble reached the veranda and hurled the young Unitarian inside.

'You're in line for the slippery dance,' someone shouted.

'Commend your soul to the devil.'

'He's as angry as a wild bull.'

'The stick will soon tame him.'

'He needs softening up.'

'First the rod and shears.'

'Or else the candle.'

'The corn-cob would be better.'

'Be silent and sit down!' ordered the judge, lowering himself into his big chair.

Everyone obeyed. The young man, still standing, glared at him.

'Vile murderers, what do you intend to do with me?' he cried, his voice charged with indignation.

'Calm down!' said the judge, smiling. 'There's no need to get worked up. You'll find out in good time.'

The young man was beside himself with rage. His whole body seemed to convulse. His livid face, his voice, his quivering lips betrayed the pounding of his heart and the state of his nerves. His fiery eyes seemed to burst from their sockets, his lank black hair bristled. His bare throat and shirt front revealed the violent throb of his arteries and his anxious breathing.

'You're trembling, are you?' asked the judge.

'Only with rage, since I can't strangle you with my bare hands.'

'Would you be strong or bold enough for it?'

'More than enough for you, you coward.'

'Let's have the shears for clipping my horse. Trim this fellow Federalist-style.'

Two men seized the Unitarian, one by the rope that bound his arms, the other by the head, and in a minute – to the onlookers' noisy laughter – they snipped off his side-whiskers, which reached all the way down to his chin.

'Fetch a glass of water to cool him down,' said the judge.

'I'd make you drink gall, you wretch,' the young man said.

A small black lackey stepped forward, a glass of water in his hand. The young man lashed out with a kick, and the glass smashed against a roof beam, showering the astonished spectators with fragments.

'He's incorrigible.'

'We'll tame him.'

'Silence!' said the judge. 'Now you're shaven like a Federalist, all you need is a moustache. See you don't forget it. Let's take stock then. Why aren't you wearing a ribbon?'

'Because I don't choose to.'

'Don't you know the Restorer demands it?'

'Livery is for slaves like you, not for free men.'

'Free men can be forced to wear it.'

'Yes, forced by bestial violence. That's your

weapon, you scoundrels. Wolves, tigers, and panthers are also strong. The lot of you should be crawling about on all fours like them.'

'Aren't you afraid the tigers will tear you to pieces?'

'I'd rather that than have my hands tied behind me while you pluck out my intestines one by one like a horde of crows.'

'Why aren't you wearing a mourning band on your hat for our heroine?'

'Because I wear one in my heart for our whole country – the country your despicable henchmen have murdered!'

'Don't you know the Restorer has decreed it?'

'No, it was you slaves who decreed it so as to flatter your lord and master's pride and pay him the tribute of cringing servitude.'

'Insolent dog, you've grown brazen. Another peep out of you and I'll have your tongue. Take down this foppish dandy's breeches and give his buttocks a taste of the rod. Bind him to the table.'

Barely had the judge spoken, when four of his blood-spattered bullies lifted the young man and stretched him out the length of the table, holding all his limbs down.

'Slit my throat rather than strip me, you blackguards.'

They gagged him and tore at his clothes. The young man squirmed, kicked out, gnashed his teeth. First his limbs were supple as a reed, then hard as iron, and his spine writhed like a snake. Drops of sweat big as pearls ran down his face; his eyes shot fire, his mouth foam, and the veins of his neck and forehead stood out dark, as if choked with blood, against his white skin.

'Tie him down first,' ordered the judge.

'He's fuming,' said one of the torturers.

A moment later, turning his body over, they bound his feet to the legs of the table. In order to do the same with his arms, they loosened the rope that held his hands behind his back. Feeling them free, the young man made a sudden movement that seemed to drain him of all his strength and vitality. He raised himself first on his arms, then on his knees, and then collapsed, murmuring, 'Slit my throat rather than strip me, you blackguards.'

His resistance gone, he was quickly tied in the form of a cross, and his tormentors continued the work of stripping off his clothes. At that, a stream of blood gushed from the young man's mouth and nostrils, and, spreading out, poured down on either side of the table. The four who had bound him stood rooted with shock; the onlookers were stunned.

'The barbarous Unitarian has burst with anger,' said one.

'He had a river of blood in his veins,' said another.

'Poor devil, all we wanted was to have fun with him, and he took it too seriously,' put in the judge, furrowing his tigerish brow. 'We'll draw up a report. Untie him and let's be off.'

The men obeyed. The door was locked, and within moments the mob had skulked off in the wake of the judge, who rode in silence and with bowed head.

The Federalists had carried out another of their many deeds of heroism. At that period, the cut-throats of the slaughteryard were the apostles who by rod and fist spread the gospel of the rosy federation, and it is not hard to imagine the sort of federation that would spring from these butchers' heads and knives. In accordance with the cant invented by the Restorer, patron of their brotherhood, they dubbed 'barbarous Unitarian' anyone who was not a barbarian, a butcher, a cut-throat, or a thief; anyone who was decent or whose heart was in the right place; every illustrious patriot or friend of enlightenment and freedom. From the events related above, it can clearly be seen that the hotbed of the Federation was in the slaughteryard.

GLOSSARY

Although firmly rooted in a particular period of Argentine history, 'The Slaughteryard' is nonetheless a work of the imagination and as such is perhaps best read on pages unencumbered with a translator's or editor's explanatory notes. The present English version has been designed for a general public, or what was once known as the common reader. (In the present age of breezy semi-literacy, perhaps the accurate term would be the *un*common reader – a member of the minority who approach books for more than mere entertainment.) The background of Echeverría's story is so rich in lore little known by readers today, including Argentine readers, that for anyone wishing to delve more deeply a guide to certain elements of the tale – in particular, its historical fabric – may not be amiss. Without having been signalled in the text proper, the words or topics that follow, together with page numbers, are presented in the order in which they occur in the narrative.

Federalists, Unitarians, Restorer, pp. 3 and 5. After six years (1810–16) of fruitless military effort to incorporate the outlying provinces of the old Viceroyalty of the Río de la Plata – Uruguay, Paraguay, and Bolivia – the provinces of modern-day Argentina determined to declare their own independence from Spain. But as the jealousies and antagonisms deepened between liberal Buenos Aires intellectuals and the people of the interior, the search for a viable form of government became more and more elusive. The delegates to the 1816 Tucumán Congress, who signed the independence act, appointed an interim supreme dictator while they went about looking for a king. The supreme dictator ruled until 1819. Meanwhile, the power of local bosses, the caudillos, who held sway over their bands of gaucho cavalry, had so increased that it soon became apparent that they would oppose king, dictator, or president. When, in 1819, the congress drafted a highly centralist constitution, the provincial caudillos opposed it.

The next fifteen years were fraught with disunity, chaos, and civil war. In this period, the two great factions arose: the Unitarians (*unitarios*), who favoured a centralist government under Buenos Aires leadership, with liberal institutions and a programme of free trade, foreign investment, and immigration; and the Federalists (*federales*), who demanded local autonomy and at the same time recognition by Buenos Aires of their rights in the national partnership. The economic basis of Federalist policy, the more primitive one of cattle production for the export of hides and salt meat, appealed to conservative, or traditionalist, values. While the Unitarians, who included a large part of the wealthy and cultured families of Buenos Aires, were clear in their stand, the Federalists were split between mutually suspicious provincial caudillos and the Buenos Aires party. Federalism, for each of these factions, proved to hold different meanings, and by the end of Rosas' reign it was little more than a cover for the self-serving sectionalism of the capital and the wealthy landowners of Buenos Aires province.

Out of this upheaval of the 1820s, in the search for a man strong enough to crush all opposition, came Juan Manuel de Rosas. Born in 1793 to a prominent Buenos Aires family, he grew up on the pampa on his father's cattle-breeding estate, of which he became manager at the age of sixteen. Competent, strict but just with his gauchos, by the age of twenty-five Rosas was a large landowner and cattle breeder, and by 1820 a powerful caudillo. With his small army, dressed by him in red (which became the colour of the Federalists), he began to intervene in politics; in 1829, he marched on Buenos Aires to put down an uprising, and in the outcome he was installed as governor. As a result of intense political intrigue, Rosas had become the chosen instrument of a powerful group of landowners in the province of Buenos Aires who were convinced that their well-being would be insured if control of the province and domination of the nation's major port were vested in one of their own number. Rosas' immediate policy was the punishment of his enemies and the demand of total submission to the Federalist party. The purge of Unitarian army chiefs began; some were shot, others jailed, and the wearing of a red ribbon by all Argentines became obligatory. His term up in 1832, Rosas refused re-election when the legislature would not extend his dictatorial powers, and for the next three years he dedicated himself to extending the borders of the province into Indian territory to the south and west of Buenos Aires. During this expedition, 6,000 hostiles were killed. Meanwhile, in the capital, Rosas' wife, doña Encarnación Ezcurra, worked hard for his return; in an effort to stage an uprising, she founded a terrorist organization known as the Mazorca, which aroused popular support for Rosas and intimidated his opposition. Three weak governors floundered in power, until at last the legislative council begged Rosas to return. He did

– on his own terms: 'total power ... for as long as he thinks necessary'.

Installed again in 1835, for the next seventeen years Rosas ruled the country with an iron hand. The terror spread, and the dictator was proclaimed 'Restorer of the Laws'. In the streets at night, the watchmen called out the hours with the chant, 'Long live the Federation! Death to the barbarous Unitarians!' This was repeated in the press, from the pulpit, and in the schools. Of this terror, an American resident reported: 'I have seen guards at mid-day enter the houses of citizens and either destroy or bear off the furniture ..., turning the families into the streets, and committing other acts of violence too horrible to mention.' In the marketplace, he continued, 'Rosas hung the bodies of many of his victims; sometimes decorating them in mockery, with ribands of the unitarian blue and even attaching to the corpses, labels, on which were inscribed the words "Beef with the hide".'

Ironically, though Rosas never took a grander title than Governor of Buenos Aires, his rule was far more centralist than the Unitarians had ever dreamed. In his foreign policy, he engaged the country in a war with Bolivia (1837–9); intervened in the affairs of Uruguay throughout the 1830s and

1840s; got himself into a costly war with France (1838-40); and suffered a blockade at the hands of an Anglo-French force (1845-48). Finally, by 1852, he had lost his support. A rival caudillo, with Brazilian and Uruguayan aid, marched upon Buenos Aires and on the third of February defeated Rosas' army at Monte Caseros, on the western outskirts of Buenos Aires. Resigning as governor, the dictator fled and was carried into exile aboard a British warship. He settled on a small Southampton farm, where he died in 1877.

But the old discord went deep, and irrationality – or barbarism – still has its champions in present-day Argentina. In 1969, Borges felt compelled to write that the revisionism of Argentine history then in vogue was not 'to get at truth but to reach a foregone conclusion – the justification of Rosas or of any other convenient despot.'

The Restorer's remains, which were repatriated in 1989, now lie in the Recoleta cemetery.

May revolution, p. 10. The May revolution, which reached a culmination on 25 May 1810, is the name given to a series of events that broke up the Viceroyalty of the Río de la Plata and brought an end to Spanish colonial rule in what is now Argentina. To Echeverría's generation, inspired by new French literary and intellectual currents, the May revolution represented an awakening from a stagnant past and held out the promise of regeneration. To him the words 'May', 'progress', and 'democracy' were synonymous. In Rosas' despotic and absolutist rule, Echeverría and other members of the Generation of 1837 saw a return to the isolation and prejudices of the colonial era. Spain at the beginning of the nineteenth century, Echeverría once wrote, was the most backward nation in Europe.

sketch, p. 11. Commentators – beginning with the first of them, Juan María Gutiérrez, in 1871 – like to label 'The Slaughteryard' as an example of what the Spanish-speaking world calls a *cuadro de costumbres*. The term, lacking a clear-cut definition, is not helpful. Trying to pinpoint one himself, Gutiérrez variously speaks of 'a typical scene' (*una escena característica*) and the 'customs' (*costumbres*) of a particular time or place; finally he plumps for the designation *cuadro de costumbres*, which is perhaps best translated as 'a picture of everyday life'. The analogous term in the critical vocabulary of the English-speaking world is 'local colour', which lays emphasis on the setting as characteristic of a time or place and reproduces customs, dialect, and costumes. The art term 'genre painting' also comes to mind. But in common with all ground-breaking works that later become classics, Echeverría's tale – which embraces a range of styles from the romantic to the realistic to the naturalistic – transcends narrow pigeon-holing.

ñandubay, p. 12. A tree (*Prosopis affinis* [syn. *nandubey*]) that grows in north-east Argentina, chiefly in Entre Ríos. Noted for its durability, the wood does not rot in contact with the soil or with water, hence its use for fence posts, stockades, and palisades.

uprising against Balcarce, p. 13. The revolt of October 1833 that unseated Rosas' successor, Juan Ramón Balcarce, and that two years later led to Rosas' return to power. Doña Encarnación Ezcurra, the Restorer's wife and tireless collaborator, was a leading figure in the machinations of this period.

Mazorca, p. 13. Among several definitions, the word *mazorca* means the fruiting spike of a cereal such as wheat or maize. In the Argentine it is the sun-dried ear of maize, as distinguished from *choclo*, which is fresh maize. Notoriously, the *mazorca* (or *Mazorca*) is also the name of the terrorist organization at the service of Rosas' government – what has aptly been termed his shock troops, recruited among the rougher elements of society and used as an instrument of State terror to intimidate all opposition. According to some historians, it is a widely held misconception that the Mazorca is the common name – or another name – for the Sociedad Popular Restauradora, an elite group of some two hundred ardent Buenos Aires Federalists, which acted as parapolice. In fact, the People's Restoration Society used the Mazorca to enforce its programme of rooting out and persecuting Unitarians as well as members of the various factions of anti-Rosas Federalists. Opponents of Rosas, especially during the time his regime flourished, tended to blur the distinction between the two organizations. Ricardo Salvatore, writing in *Revolución, República, Confederación (1806–1852)*, the third volume of a recent multi-tomed history of the Argentine, elaborates as follows:

… the Mazorca performed the work of intimidation and political assassination ordered by that Society. By night, *mazorqueros* rode through the city, firing shots at the windows or walls of the houses of those suspected of opposing the regime, with the object of terrifying the occupants. It was also a common practice to raid particular homes in search of incriminating evidence. In general, those singled out by one means or another saved their skins by choosing the path of exile. After several such warnings, assassins would come calling. The *mazorqueros'* preferred method was to cut their victims' throats with a knife, an act performed after they had been submitted to sadistic, degrading rituals in which they were treated like women. At the height of the wave of terror, in August 1845, headless corpses could be found every morning in the streets of Buenos Aires.

The cryptic words 'treated like women' probably refer to three lines in Hilario Ascasubi's famous poem 'La refalosa'. Here a *mazorquero* describes kissing in mockery a victim whose throat has been slit. For the most part, however, commentators speak only in general terms of 'torture' and 'abuse' and are otherwise silent or guarded or reticent about the sexual nature of certain of the Mazorca's acts. Not so Rosas' foremost critic, Domingo F. Sarmiento, who is blunt and specific. He wrote in 1849 (*Obras completas*, VI, 245) of Rosas' unruly followers, who had been 'organized under the name of the People's Society, later called the Mazorca, because of Rosas' present to them of a great ear of maize, decked out in red ribbons, which they could "stick up the barbarous Unitarians" – the exact words of the message with which General Rosas accompanied the gift.' Sarmiento records as well (*Facundo*, 1845 edition, p. 265) that the Mazorca also softened up its victims with enemas of chili pepper or turpentine.

Mazorca is often spelled *mashorca* – with or without a capital – and pronounced in the same way as *mazorca*. The writer Lucio Mansilla maintained that anyone who wrote the word in the form *mas horca* was mistaken. Consistently, both Ascasubi and Echeverría spelled it thus. In this usage, broken into components, there is the obvious play on words, and the term translates as 'more gibbets' – that is, more hangings, more assassinations, more throat-cutting or beheading. Echeverría defines the *mas-horca* as 'a band of assassins, thieves, and throat-slitters' and speaks of the group's 'all-too-meaningful name' (see p. 156). The reference to theft alludes to the confiscation of country estates, or estancias, which were retained for the use of Federalist troops but whose furniture and goods were sold at public auction, with the proceeds distributed among those who had contributed to the Federalist cause. A primitive water-colour of the period depicts a scene, outside the walls of the

Recoleta cemetery, in which a family lies with slit throats while a corpse is being robbed of a watch by one of four assassins. In his novel *Amalia* (1855), José Mármol describes in documentary detail (I, 13) a meeting of the People's Restoration Society, 'the union of whose members was symbolized by an ear of maize, in imitation of an old Spanish organization that used the same emblem and whose object was the propagation of *Más-horca* [more gallows] – a mistaken pronunciation which helped define the symbol and idea, and was also applied to the People's Society of Buenos Aires.' Another source suggests that the ear of maize stood for the unity of Rosas' Federalists, who were as close as the kernels in an ear of maize. In Chile, the word *mazorca* is used for a junta that forms a despotic government.

Readers of *Nunca Más*, the 1984 report of the Argentine National Commission on Missing Persons, will find immediate and disturbing parallels between the techniques of Rosas' Mazorca and those of his successors in the military dictatorship that ruled the country from 1976 to 1983. Even the name of the 1970s phenomenon, the so-called Process of National Reorganization, has a bureaucratic tang akin to that of the words Sociedad Popular Restauradora.

Assessments of the number of victims of Rosas' reign of terror from 1829 to 1852 vary widely. The main sources are three:

(1) José Rivera Indarte's so-called 'Tables of Blood', compiled for the years 1829–43. These list 3,765 throats cut, 1,293 shootings, and 722 assassinations. They also include 14,920 killed in battle and 1,600 killed in other actions or for desertion. The grand total in this summation is 22,404. John Lynch, Rosas' 1981 biographer, considers these figures 'biased and probably too high.'

(2) The official figures, also for the period 1829–43, compiled in refutation of Rivera Indarte by the pro-Rosas *Gaceta Mercantil*. These total 500 and break down as follows: executions in other provinces, 250; Indians executed after capture, 100; and Unitarians executed,150.

(3) The figures, from 1829 to 1852, compiled for Rosas' trial in absentia, in 1857. These give a total of 2,354.

Political executions, Lynch concludes, claimed more than 250 victims and fewer than 6,000. He settles for something 'in the region of 2,000' and goes on to say:

If the historian is unable to measure the terror, he may nonetheless draw some conclusions. These were not mass murders. The targets were precisely chosen and carefully identified. Their impact, however, is not to be measured by quantity alone, but by the suffering they inflicted on the victims' families and by the fear they instilled in the whole population…. If ever a regime ruled by the principle of fear it was this. Rosas acted according to a pure Hobbesian belief that fear is the only thing which makes men keep the laws.

The recent multi-volume history of Argentina cited earlier, more or less repeating Lynch's finding, comes up with 'a minimum of 250 and a maximum of 6,000.'

See also **corn-cob** below, p. 52.

chiripá, p. 13. The poet Ascasubi's definition is succinct – 'a countryman's garment in the form of a piece of cloth that is caught up between the legs'. According to Argentine sources, the name derives from two Quechua words meaning 'for the cold'. The article of clothing itself – which the gaucho and his successor, the *paisano*, took from the Indians – was throughout the nineteenth century the classic costume of the River Plate country dweller and cavalryman. Often worn with ankle-length white drawers known as *calzoncillos*, the *chiripá* is sumptuously depicted in the work of painters like Juan León Pallière and Raimundo

Quinsac Monvoisin. The garment was eventually replaced by the wide baggy trousers known as *bombachas*.

The term *gente de chiripá*, as used among refined city-dwellers, referred to unsophisticated rustics. In the Rosas period, the *chiripá* – standing for native, or American, values – became a symbol of Federalism in opposition to the frock coat or tail-coat worn by men of the city, who looked to European ways. Mansilla recounts that *lomonegros*, or black-backs, was the epithet Rosas gave to city dwellers who wore such dress. Distinctions in dress at this time were also reflected in the style of men's facial hair, the Unitarians favouring a U-shaped beard and the Federalists a bushy moustache and side whiskers. A number of elements in Echeverría's story further elaborate the dichotomy: pistols versus the knife, the English saddle versus the local *recado*. In more abstract terms, the list can be drawn out to include culture versus ignorance, Buenos Aires versus the provinces, and ultimately and most famously Sarmiento's all-embracing distinction, civilization versus barbarism.

Some Argentines claim the *chiripá* is a unique garment, but it is very much akin to the Hindu dhoti, or loincloth.

ox carts, p. 14. The ox, or bullock, cart is richly
depicted in the iconography of nineteenth-century
Buenos Aires. Beginning with the work of Fernando Brambila, in the 1790s, a host of artists,
working in all media – etchings, water-colours,
aquatints, lithographs, drawings, oils – carefully
documented the various *carros, carretas*, and *carritos*, two-wheeled carts of different sizes, used in the
transport of people and goods. The best of these
artists include Emeric Essex Vidal, César Hipólito
Bacle, Carlos Enrique Pellegrini, Gregorio Ibarra
(whose butcher's cart is pulled by two horses),
Juan León Pallière, Juan Mauricio Rugendas,
Pridiliano Pueyrredón, and Carlos Morel.

In his *Picturesque Illustrations of Buenos
Aires...*, Vidal pointed out that 'There are no
waggons at Buenos Aires; all carriages of burden
move on two high wheels.' Apparently unaware
of the distinction in terminology, Darwin noted
on a journey from Buenos Aires to Santa Fe (27
September 1833): 'These waggons are very long,
narrow, and thatched with reeds; they have only
two wheels, the diameter of which in some cases
is even 10 feet. Each is drawn by six bullocks
which are urged on by a goad at least 20 feet
long: this is suspended from within the roof; for
the wheel bullocks a small one is kept; and for the

intermediate pair, a point projects at right angles from the middle of the long one. The whole apparatus looked like some implement of war.'

Darwin's is the classical description of the *carreta*, a slightly smaller version of which had been plying the pampa since the first convoys began travelling between Buenos Aires and Salta in about 1595. That journey, of nearly 1,000 miles, took three months.

The *carro* was a smaller and squatter vehicle, and smaller still were the *carritos*, which were used within the city by water-sellers and butchers, among others. These carts were sometimes drawn by horses.

The *carreta* was analogous to the prairie schooner of the United States.

lassos, p. 14. Argentine horsemanship came from Spain via the conquistadores and derives from the riding style of a Berber tribe, the *zenetes* or *xenetes*, who once served in the Granada cavalry. In a country like Argentina, known for its horses and for the riding skills of its gauchos and *paisanos*, it is only natural that every article of riding gear and apparel has been subjected to minute and lengthy study, so that entire specialized handbooks and dictionaries are devoted to the subject. One such detailed vocabulary, for example, defines the word *lunanco* as 'a horse or mule which from birth or as the result of a blow has one hip bone lower than the other.' And so too with the distinctions attached to the lasso and to the roping of livestock. The Argentines have two different verbs for lassoing animals. *Enlazar* is to rope a cow by the horns or a horse by the neck; *pialar* is to rope an animal by its forelegs, and in this instance the lariat is usually thrown by a man on foot. There are also numerous terms for throwing the *pial*, according to whether the animal is roped from the left or right side, from behind or over its back, whether the rope – twisted or braided rawhide anything from twelve to twenty-five metres long – is or is not twirled. And then there are the various combinations and permutations.

Lassos have traditionally been made of the hide of the cow, guanaco, stag, jackass, and the sinew of the rhea or the bull. The lasso used in slaughter-yards and the meat-salting establishments was of a shorter length than that used on the open plain.

corn-cob, p. 25. The corn-cob, or *mazorca*, was both the symbol of Rosas' terrorist organization and the instrument of torture and humiliation used for the anal rape of its victims.

In 1845, a British general had disclosed to the British statesman Lord Aberdeen that the 'Mashorca, or secret affiliation in support of Rosas' government, derives its name from the inward stalk of the maize, when deprived of its grain, and has been used by the members of the club as an instrument of torture of which your lordship may have some idea when calling to mind the agonising death inflicted upon Edward II.'

Ten years earlier, Echeverría's biographer and editor Juan María Gutiérrez had written that the Mazorca's objective was 'to introduce into the backside of the Unitarian enemy the tasty fruit from which the organization derived its name; as a result, all those in fear of such a misfortune have taken to wearing tight-fitting trousers, thereby using fashion to mask a measure both sensible and prudent'.

See also **Mazorca** above, p. 42.

violin, p. 26. *Violín y violón*, meaning violin and double-bass, was the slang term used in the time of Rosas for slitting a person or an animal's throat or neck. The word music and the grim humour of the Spanish are lost in translation. To play the violin was a simile comparing the action of drawing a knife across the throat with that of drawing a bow across a stringed instrument. The standard word, *degollar*, to cut the throat, also means to behead or decapitate. Ascasubi notes that Colonel Vicente Maza, a *mashorquero* and favourite of Rosas, was variously nicknamed Violón, Maza Violín, Maza Violón, and don Violón; and that a *mashorquero* cut-throat was known as a *tropa violinista*, or soldier-violinist.

In a couple of astonishing pages, W.H. Hudson (*Far Away and Long Ago*, VIII) tells of a band of veteran Federalist soldiers – in flight after Rosas' fall in the battle of Caseros – slitting the throat of their young officer:

… it was a common thing in the case of a defeat in those days for the men to turn upon and murder their officers. Nor was throat-cutting a mere custom or convention: to the old soldier it was the only satisfactory way of finishing off your adversary, or prisoner of war, or your officer who had been your tyrant, on the day of defeat…. And so in those dark times in the Argentine Republic when … the people of the plains had developed an amazing ferocity, they loved to kill a man not with a bullet but in a manner to make them know and feel that they were really and truly killing.

… as time went on and I heard more about this painful subject I began to realise what it meant. The full horror of it came only a few years later, when I was big enough to go about to the native houses and among the gauchos in their gatherings, at cattle-partings and brandings, races, and on other occasions. I listened to the conversation of groups of men whose lives had been mostly spent in the army, as a rule in guerilla warfare, and the talk turned with surprising frequency to the subject of cutting throats. Not to waste powder on prisoners was an unwritten law of the Argentine army at that period, and the veteran gaucho clever with the knife took delight in obeying it. It always came as a relief, I heard them say, to have as victim a young man with a good neck after an experience of tough, scraggy old throats: with a person of that sort they were in no hurry to finish the business; it was performed in a leisurely, loving way. Darwin, writing in praise of the gaucho in his *Voyage of a Naturalist*, says that if a gaucho cuts your throat he does it like a gentleman: even as a small boy I knew better – that he did his business rather like a hellish creature revelling in his cruelty. He would listen to all his captive could say to soften his heart – all his heartrending prayers and pleadings; and would reply: "Ah, friend," – or little friend, or brother – "your words pierce me to the heart and I would gladly spare you for the sake of that poor mother of yours who fed you with her milk, and for your own sake too, since in this short time I have conceived a great friendship towards you; but your beautiful neck is your undoing, for how could I possibly deny myself the pleasure of cutting such a throat – so shapely, so smooth and soft and so white!

Think of the sight of warm red blood gushing from that white column!" And so on, with wavings of the steel blade before the captive's eyes, until the end.

When I heard them relate such things – and I am quoting their very words, remembered all these years only too well – laughingly, gloating over such memories, such a loathing and hatred possessed me that ever afterwards the very sight of these men was enough to produce a sensation of nausea, just as when in the dog days one inadvertently rides too near the putrid carcass of some large beast on the plain.

Ascasubi records that heads were also severed with handsaws.

slippery dance, p. 27. *La refalosa* (or *resbalosa*) was the name of an old dance that became popular among Federalists in Rosas' time. The Mazorca sometimes accompanied a public spectacle of throat-cutting with the music of this dance. The victim would be made to stand stark naked, bound hand and foot or held in the grip of several *mazorqueros*, and then let loose to slip and slide in imitation of dancing in the blood that streamed from his slit throat. A graphic description of the procedure is found in Ascasubi's famous poem 'La refalosa'. (See Appendix 6, p. 141.)

Echeverría wrote that 'The *Resvalosa* is a sonata of throat-cutting, and, as the word itself indicates, it enacts the sliding movement of a knife blade across a victim's throat and is sung and danced at the same time.' Crediting Rosas with having invented the *Resvalosa*, Echeverría cites his ingenuity as an example of 'the Federalist burlesque style'. (See Appendix 7, p. 151.) Hudson (*Far Away and Long Ago*, VIII) remarks of Rosas' temperament that 'There were many other acts which to foreigners and to those born in later times might seem the result of insanity, but which were really the outcome of a peculiar, sardonic, and somewhat primitive sense of humour on his part which appeals powerfully to the men of the plains, the gauchos, among whom Rosas lived from boyhood ... and by whose aid he eventually rose to supreme power.'

EL MATADERO
THE ORIGINAL TEXT

The manuscript of 'El matadero' has not survived. All we know about it is contained in a brief remark by Juan María Gutiérrez in his foreword to the first printing of the story, in 1871. There, he comments on the shakiness of the author's handwriting, 'which is barely legible in the original'.

In the absence of an ur-text, subsequent compilers and commentators have had to rely on Gutiérrez's first edition and on his revision of it, in 1874, for Vol. V of Echeverría's *Obras completas*. But editing practices in nineteenth-century Argentina were notoriously haphazard. Gutiérrez failed to correct certain errors in the first printing and introduced fresh errors into the second. Since then, efforts to establish a text of 'El matadero' have mainly consisted of collating the two early printings and introducing modernized spelling, punctuation, and use of accents.

The text presented here is that of the first printed version of the story as it appeared in the *Revista del Río de la Plata*, Vol. I, No. 4, Buenos Aires, 1871, pp. 563–85. Except for five bracketed interpolations, each of which corrects a mistake in the preceding word, what follows is virtually a transcription of the initial printing. Inconsistencies of spelling, capitalization, and punctuation as well as errors of punctuation are all here reproduced. Idiosyncratic personal and local usage has been respected. Accents, or their absence, follow the style of the original. Missing upside-down interrogation and exclamation marks have not been supplied. (In two places only does the 1871 edition provide these.) Duck-foot quotes, or guillemets, have been retained, and even a wrongly italicized semicolon.

The aim has been to bring the reader closer to Echeverría and his period, to give a flavour of practices in Spanish spelling from an era before the rules were fixed, and to present a text that it is otherwise difficult to come by. Readers may draw their own conclusion as to who supplied the ellipses – author or editor? – after the first letter of the five or six vulgar words found in the story's dialogue. Without an ur-text we will never know for sure. Ironically, the handwritten pages survived for twenty or more years after the author's death. Echeverría himself once remarked that the correction and revision of a manuscript inspired in him 'invincible repugnance'.

The main text, in the original printing, appeared under the heading given below and was preceded by Gutiérrez's foreword (see Appendix 1, p. 95). The story itself followed the inexplicable Roman numeral I.

EL MATADERO.

POR DON ESTEBAN ECHEVERRIA.

(Inédito.)

I.

Apesar de que la mia es historia, no la empezaré por el arca de Noé y la genealogia de sus ascendientes como acostumbraban hacerlo los antiguos historiadores españoles de América que deben ser nuestros prototipos. Tengo muchas razones para no seguir ese ejemplo, las que callo por no ser difuso. Diré solamente que los sucesos de mi narracion, pasaban por los años de Cristo de 183.... Estábamos, á mas, en cuaresma, época en que escasea la carne en Buenos Aires, porque la iglesia adoptando el precepto de Epitecto [Epicteto], *sustine abstine* (sufre, abstente) ordena vigilia y abstinencia á los estómagos de los fieles, á causa de que la carne es pecaminosa, y, como dice el proverbio, busca á la carne. Y como la iglesia tiene *ab initio* y por delegacion directa de Dios el imperio inmaterial sobre las conciencias y estómagos, que en manera alguna pertenecen al individuo, nada mas justo y racional que vede lo malo.

Los abastecedores, por otra parte, buenos federales, y por lo mismo buenos católicos, sabiendo que el pueblo de Buenos Aires atesora una docilidad singular para someterse á toda especie de mandamiento, solo traen en dias cuaresmales al matadero, los novillos necesarios para el sustento de los niños y de los enfermos dispensados de la abstinencia por la Bula.... y no con el ánimo de que se harten algunos herejotes, que no faltan, dispuestos siempre á violar los mandamientos carnificinos de la iglesia, y á contaminar la sociedad con el mal ejemplo.

Sucedió, pues, en aquel tiempo, una lluvia muy copiosa. Los caminos se anegaron; los pantanos se pusieron á nado y las calles de entrada y salida á la ciudad rebosaban en acuoso barro. Una tremenda avenida se precipitó de repente por el Riachuelo de Barracas, y estendió magestuosamente sus turbias aguas hasta el pié de las barrancas del alto. El Plata creciendo embravecido empujó esas aguas que venian buscando su cauce y las hizo correr hinchadas por sobre campos, terraplenes, arboledas, caserios, y estenderse como un lago inmenso por todas las bajas tierras. La ciudad circunvalada del Norte al Este por una cintura de agua y barro, y al Sud por un piélago blanquecino en cuya superficie flotaban á la ventura algunos barquichuelos y negreaban

las chimeneas y las copas de los árboles, echaba
desde sus torres y barrancas atónitas miradas al
horizonte como implorando misericordia al Altísimo. Parecia el amago de un nuevo diluvio. Los
beatos y beatas gimoteaban haciendo novenarios
y contínuas plegarias. Los predicadores atronaban
el templo y hacian crujir el púlpito á puñetazos.
Es el dia del juicio, decian, el fin del mundo está
por venir. La cólera divina rebosando se derrama
en inundacion. Ay! de vosotros pecadores! Ay!
de vosotros unitarios impíos que os mofais de la
iglesia, de los santos, y no escuchais con venera-
cion la palabra de los ungidos del Señor! Ah de
vosotros si no implorais misericordia al pié de los
altares! Llegará la hora tremenda del vano crujir de
dientes y de las frenéticas imprecaciones. Vuestra
impiedad, vuestras heregias, vuestras blasfemias,
vuestros crímenes horrendos, han traido sobre
nuestra tierra las plagas del Señor. La justicia y el
Dios de la Federacion os declarará malditos.

Las pobres mujeres salian sin aliento, anonadadas
del templo, echando, como era natural, la culpa de
aquella calamidad á los unitarios.

Continuaba, sin embargo, lloviendo á cántaros,
y la inundacion crecia acreditando el pronóstico
de los predicadores. Las campanas comenzaron
á tocar rogativas por órden del muy católico

Restaurador, quien parece no las tenia todas consigo. Los libertinos, los incrédulos, es decir, los unitarios, empezaron á amedrentarse al ver tanta cara compungida, oir tanta batahola de imprecaciones. Se hablaba ya como de cosa resuelta de una procesion en que debia ir toda la poblacion descalza y á cráneo descubierto, acompañando al Altísimo, llevado bajo pálio por el Obispo, hasta la barranca de Balcarce, donde millares de voces conjurando al demonio unitario de la inundacion, debian implorar la misericordia divina.

Feliz, ó mejor, desgraciadamente, pues la cosa habria sido de verse, no tuvo efecto la ceremonia, porque bajando el Plata, la inundacion se fué poco á poco escurriendo en su inmenso lecho sin necesidad de conjuro ni plegarias.

Lo que hace principalmente á mi historia es que por causa de la inundacion estuvo quince dias el matadero de la Convalescencia sin ver una sola cabeza vacuna, y que en uno ó dos, todos los bueyes de quinteros y *aguateros* se consumieron en el abasto de la ciudad. Los pobres niños y enfermos se alimentaban con huevos y gallinas, y los gringos y herejotes bramaban por el beef-steak y el asado. La abstinencia de carne era general en el pueblo, que nunca se hizo mas digno de la bendicion de la iglesia, y así fué que llovieron sobre él millones y millones de indulgencias plenarias. Las gallinas se pusieron á 6 $ y los huevos á 4 reales y el pescado carísimo. No hubo en aquellas [aquellos] dias cuaresmales promiscuaciones ni excesos de gula; pero en cambio se fueron derecho al cielo innumerables ánimas y acontecieron cosas que parecen soñadas.

No quedó en el matadero ni un solo raton vivo de muchos millares que allí tenian albergue. Todos murieron ó de hambre ó ahogados en sus cuevas por la incesante lluvia. Multitud de negras rebusconas de *achuras*, como los caranchos de presa, se desbandaron por la ciudad como otras tantas harpías prontas á devorar cuanto hallaran comible. Las gaviotas y los perros inseparables rivales suyos en el matadero, emigraron en busca de alimento animal. Porcion de viejos achacosos cayeron en consuncion por falta de nutritivo caldo; pero lo mas notable que sucedió fué el fallecimiento casi repentino de unos cuantos gringos herejes que cometieron el desacato de darse un hartazgo de chorizos de estremadura, jamon y bacalao y se fueron al otro mundo á pagar el pecado cometido por tan abominable promiscuacion.

Algunos médicos opinaron que si la carencia de carne continuaba, medio pueblo caeria en síncope por estar los estómagos acostumbrados á su corroborante jugo; y era de notar el contraste entre estos tristes pronósticos de la ciencia y los anatemas lanzados desde el púlpito por los reverendos padres contra toda clase de nutricion animal y de promiscuacion en aquellos dias destinados por la iglesia al ayuno y la penitencia. Se originó de aquí una especie de guerra intestina entre los estómagos y las conciencias, atizada por el inexorable apetito y las no menos inexorables vociferaciones de los ministros de la iglesia, quienes, como es su deber, no transigen con vicio alguno que tienda á relajar las costumbres católicas: á lo que se agregaba el estado de flatulencia intestinal de los habitantes, producido por el pescado y los porotos y otros alimentos algo indigestos.

Esta guerra se manifestaba por sollozos y gritos descompasados en la peroracion de los sermones y por rumores y estruendos subitáneos en las casas y calles de la ciudad ó donde quiera concurrian gentes. Alarmóse un tanto el gobierno, tan paternal como previsor, del Restaurador creyendo aquellos tumultos de orígen revolucionario y atribuyéndolos á los mismos salvajes unitarios, cuyas impiedades, segun los predicadores federales, habian traido sobre el pais la inundacion de la cólera divina; tomó activas providencias, desparramó sus esbirros por la poblacion y por último, bien informado, promulgó un decreto tranquilizador de las conciencias y de los estómagos, encabezado por un considerando muy sábio y piadoso para que á todo trance y arremetiendo por agua y todo se trajese ganado á los corrales.

En efecto, el décimo sesto dia de la carestia víspera del dia de Dolores, entró á nado por el paso de Burgos al matadero del Alto una tropa de cincuenta novillos gordos; cosa poca por cierto para una poblacion acostumbrada á consumir diariamente de 250 á 300, y cuya tercera parte al menos gozaria del fuero eclesiástico de alimentarse con carne. ¡Cosa estraña que haya estómagos privilegiados y estómagos sujetos á leyes inviolables y que la iglesia tenga la llave de los estómagos!

Pero no es estraño, supuesto que el diablo con la carne suele meterse en el cuerpo y que la iglesia tiene el poder de conjurarlo: el caso es reducir al hombre á una máquina cuyo móvil principal no sea su voluntad sino la de la iglesia y el gobierno. Quizá llegue el dia en que sea prohibido respirar aire libre, pasearse y hasta conversar con un amigo, sin permiso de autoridad competente. Así era, poco mas ó menos, en los felices tiempos de nuestros beatos abuelos que por desgracia vino á turbar la revolucion de Mayo.

Sea como fuera; á la noticia de la providencia gubernativa, los corrales del Alto se llenaron, á pesar del barro, de carniceros, achuradores y curiosos, quienes recibieron con grandes vociferaciones y palmoteos los cincuenta novillos destinados al matadero.

–Chica, pero gorda, esclamaban.–Viva la Federacion! Viva el Restaurador! Porque han de saber los lectores que en aquel tiempo la Federacion estaba en todas partes, hasta entre las inmundicias del matadero y no habia fiesta sin Restaurador como no hay sermon sin Agustin. Cuentan que al oir tan desaforados gritos las últimas ratas que agonizaban de hambre en sus cuevas, se reanimaron y echaron á correr desatentadas conociendo que volvian á aquellos lugares la acostumbrada alegria y la algazara precursora de abundancia.

El primer novillo que se mató fué todo entero de regalo al Restaurador, hombre muy amigo del asado. Una comision de carniceros marchó á ofrecérselo á nombre de los federales del matadero, manifestándole *in voce* su agradecimiento por la acertada providencia del gobierno, su adhesion ilimitada al Restaurador y su ódio entrañable á los salvajes unitarios, enemigos de Dios y de los hombres. El Restaurador contestó á la arenga *rinforzando* sobre el mismo tema y concluyó la ceremonia con los correspondientes vivas y vociferaciones de los espectadores y actores. Es de creer que el Restaurador tuviese permiso especial de su ilustrísima para no abstenerse de carne, porque siendo tan buen observador de las leyes, tan buen católico y tan acérrimo protector de la religion, no hubiera dado mal ejemplo aceptando semejante regalo en dia santo.

Siguió la matanza y en un cuarto de hora cuarenta y nueve novillos se hallan tendidos en la playa del matadero, desollados unos, los otros por desollar. El espectáculo que ofrecia entonces era animado y pintoresco aunque reunia todo lo horriblemente feo, inmundo y deforme de una pequeña clase proletaria peculiar del Rio de la Plata. Pero para que el lector pueda percibirlo á un golpe de ojo preciso es hacer un cróquis de la localidad.

El matadero de la Convalescencia ó del Alto, sito en las quintas al Sud de la ciudad, es una gran playa en forma rectangular colocada al estremo de dos calles, una de las cuales allí se termina y la otra se prolonga hácia el Este. Esta playa con declive al Sud, está cortada por un zanjon labrado por la corriente de las aguas pluviales, en cuyos bordes laterales se muestran innumerables cuevas de ratones y cuyo cauce, recoge en tiempo de lluvia, toda la sangrasa seca ó reciente del matadero. En la juncion del ángulo recto hácia el Oeste está lo que llaman la casilla, edificio bajo, de tres piezas de media agua con corredor al frente que dá á la calle y palenque para atar caballos, á cuya espalda se notan varios corrales de palo á pique de ñandubay con sus fornidas puertas para encerrar el ganado.

Estos corrales son en tiempo de invierno un verdadero lodazal en el cual los animales apeñuscados se hunden hasta el encuentro y quedan como pegados y casi sin movimiento. En la casilla se hace la recaudacion del impuesto de corrales, se cobran las multas por violacion de reglamentos y se sienta el juez del matadero, personaje importante, caudillo de los carniceros y que ejerce la suma del poder en aquella pequeña república por delegacion del Restaurador.–Facil es calcular qué clase de hombre se requiere para el desempeño de semejante cargo. La casilla por otra parte, es un edificio tan ruin y pequeño que nadie lo notaria en los corrales á no estar asociado su nombre al del terrible juez y á no resaltar sobre su blanca cintura los siguientes letreros rojos: «Viva la Federacion,» «Viva el Restaurador y la heroina doña Encarnacion Ezcurra,» «Mueran los salvajes unitarios.» Letreros muy significativos, símbolo de la fé política y religiosa de la gente del matadero. Pero algunos lectores no sabrán que la tal heroina es la difunta esposa del Restaurador, patrona muy querida de los carniceros, quienes, ya muerta, la veneraban como viva por sus virtudes cristianas y su federal heroismo en la revolucion contra Balcarce. Es el caso que en un aniversario de aquella memorable hazaña de la mazorca los carniceros festejaron con un espléndido banquete en la casilla á la heroina, banquete á que concurrió con su hija y otras señoras federales, y que allí en presencia de un gran concurso ofreció á los señores carniceros en un solemne brindis su federal patrocinio, por cuyo motivo ellos la proclamaron entusiasmados patrona del matadero, estampando su nombre en las paredes de la casilla donde se estará hasta que lo borre la mano del tiempo.

La perspectiva del matadero á la distancia era grotesca, llena de animacion. Cuarenta y nueve reses estaban tendidas sobre sus cueros y cerca de doscientas personas hollaban aquel suelo de lodo regado con la sangre de sus arterias. En torno de cada res resaltaba un grupo de figuras humanas de tez y raza distintas. La figura mas prominente de cada grupo era el carnicero con el cuchillo en mano, brazo y pecho desnudos, cabello largo y revuelto, camisa y chiripá y rostro embadurnado de sangre. A sus espaldas se rebullian caracoleando y siguiendo los movimientos una comparsa de muchachos, de negras y mulatas achuradoras, cuya fealdad trasuntaba las harpías de la fábula, y entremezclados con ella algunos enormes mastines, olfateaban, gruñian ó se daban de tarascones por la presa. Cuarenta y tantas carretas toldadas con negruzco y pelado cuero se escalonaban irregularmente á lo largo de la playa y algunos ginetes con el poncho calado y el lazo prendido al tiento, cruzaban por entre ellas al tranco ó reclinados sobre el pescuezo de los caballos echaban ojo indolente sobre uno de aquellos animados grupos, al paso que mas arriba, en el aire, un enjambre de gaviotas blanquiazules que habian vuelto de la emigracion al olor de carne, revoloteaban cubriendo con su disonante graznido todos los ruidos y voces del matadero y proyectando una sombra clara sobre aquel campo de horrible carniceria. Esto se notaba al principio de la matanza.

Pero á medida que adelantaba, la perspectiva variaba; los grupos se deshacian, venian á formarse tomando diversas aptitudes y se desparramaban corriendo como si en medio de ellos cayese alguna bala perdida ó asomase la quijada de algun encolerizado mastin. Esto era, que inter el carnicero en un grupo descuartizaba á golpe de

hacha, colgaba en otro los cuartos en los ganchos
á su carreta, despellejaba en este, sacaba el sebo en
aquel, de entre la chusma que ojeaba y aguardaba
la presa de achura salia de cuando en cuando una
mugrienta mano á dar un tarazcon con el cuchillo
al sebo ó á los cuartos de la res, lo que originaba
gritos y esplosion de cólera del carnicero y el con-
tínuo hervidero de los grupos,–dichos y griteria
descompasada de los muchachos.

–Ahí se mete el sebo en las tetas, la tia, gritaba
uno.

–Aquel lo escondió en el alzapon, replicaba la
negra.

–Che! negra bruja, salí de aquí antes que te
pegue un tajo, esclamaba el carnicero.

–Qué le hago ño, Juan? no sea malo! Yo no
quiero sino la panza y las tripas.

–Son para esa bruja: á la m.....

–A la bruja! á la bruja! repitieron los muchachos:
se lleva la riñonada y el tongorí! Y cayeron sobre
su cabeza sendos cuajos de sangre y tremendas
pelotas de barro.

Hácia otra parte, entre tanto, dos africanas lleva-
ban arrastrando las entrañas de un animal; allá
una mulata se alejaba con un ovillo de tripas y
resbalando de repente sobre un charco de sangre,
caia á plomo, cubriendo con su cuerpo la codiciada

presa. Acullá se veian acurrucadas en hilera 400 negras destegiendo sobre las faldas el ovillo y arrancando uno á uno los sebitos que el avaro cuchillo del carnicero habia dejado en la tripa como rezagados, al paso que otras vaciaban panzas y vegigas y las henchian de aire de sus pulmones para depositar en ellas, luego de secas, la achura.

Varios muchachos gambeteando á pié y á caballo se daban de vegigazos ó se tiraban bolas de carne, desparramando con ellas y su algazara la nube de gabiotas que columpiándose en el aire celebraba chillando la matanza. Oíanse á menudo á pesar del veto del Restaurador y de la santidad del dia, palabras inmundas y obscéneas [obscenas], vociferaciones preñadas de todo el cinismo bestial que caracteriza á la chusma de nuestros mataderos, con las cuales no quiero regalar á los lectores.

De repente caia un bofe sangriento sobre la cabeza de alguno, que de allí pasaba á la de otro, hasta que algun deforme mastin lo hacia buena presa, y una cuadrilla de otros, por si estrujo ó no estrujo, armaba una tremenda de gruñidos y mordiscones. Alguna tia vieja salia furiosa en persecucion de un muchacho que le habia embadurnado el rostro con sangre, y acudiendo á sus gritos y puteadas los compañeros del rapaz, la rodeaban y asuzaban como los perros al toro y llovian sobre ella zoquetes de carne, bolas de estiercol, con groseras carcajadas y gritos frecuentes, hasta que el juez mandaba restablecer el órden y despejar el campo.

Por un lado dos muchachos se adiestraban en el manejo del cuchillo tirándose horrendos tajos y reveses; por otro cuatro ya adolescentes ventilaban á cuchilladas el derecho á una tripa gorda y un mondongo que habian robado á un carnicero; y no de ellos distante, porcion de perros flacos ya de la forzosa abstinencia, empleaban el mismo medio para saber quién se llevaria un hígado envuelto en barro. Simulacro en pequeño era este del modo bárbaro con que se ventilan en nuestro pais las cuestiones y los derechos individuales y sociales. En fin, la escena que se representaba en el matadero era para vista no para escrita.

Un animal habia quedado en los corrales de corta y ancha cerviz, de mirar fiero, sobre cuyos órganos genitales no estaban conformes los pareceres porque tenia apariencias de toro y de novillo. Llególe su hora. Dos enlazadores á caballo penetraron al corral en cuyo contorno hervia la chusma á pié, á caballo y horquetada sobre sus ñudosos palos. Formaban en la puerta el mas grotesco y sobresaliente grupo varios pialadores y enlazadores de á pié con el brazo desnudo y armados del certero lazo, la cabeza cubierta con un pañuelo punzó y chaleco y chiripá colorado, teniendo á sus espaldas varios ginetes y espectadores de ojo escrutador y anhelante.

El animal prendido ya al lazo por las astas, bramaba echando espuma furibundo y no habia demonio que lo hiciera salir del pegajoso barro donde estaba como clavado y era imposible pialarlo. Gritábanlo, lo azuzaban en vano con las mantas y pañuelos los muchachos prendidos sobre las horquetas del corral, y era de oir la disonante batahola de silbidos, palmadas y voces tiples y roncas que se desprendia de aquella singular orquesta.

Los dicharachos, las esclamaciones chistosas y obscénas rodaban de boca en boca y cada cual hacia alarde espontáneamente de su ingénio y de su agudeza excitado por el espectáculo ó picado por el aguijon de alguna lengua locuaz.

–Hí de p.... en el toro.

–Al diablo los torunos del Azul.

–Mal haya el tropero que nos dá gato por liebre.

–Si es novillo.

–No está viendo que es toro viejo?

–Como toro le ha de quedar. Muéstreme los c...., si le parece, c.....o!

–Ahí los tiene entre las piernas. No los vé,

amigo, mas grandes que la cabeza de su castaño;
¿ó se ha quedado ciego en el camino?

–Su madre seria la ciega, pues que tal hijo ha
parido. No vé que todo ese bulto es barro?

–Es emperrado y arisco como un unitario. Y
al oir esta mágica palabra todos á una voz escla-
maron: mueran los salvages unitarios!

–Para el tuerto los h.....

–Sí, para el tuerto, que es hombre de c..... para
pelear con los unitarios.

–El matahambre á Matasiete, degollador de
unitarios. Viva Matasiete!

–A Matasiete el matahambre!

–Allá vá, gritó una voz ronca interrumpiendo
aquellos desahogos de la cobardia feroz. Allá vá
el toro!

–Alerta! Guarda los de la puerta. Allá vá furioso
como un demonio!

Y en efecto, el animal acosado por los gritos y
sobre todo por dos picanas agudas que le espo-
leaban la cola, sintiendo flojo el lazo, arremetió
bufando á la puerta, lanzando á entrambos lados
una rógiza y fosfórica mirada. Dióle el tiron el
enlazador sentando su caballo, desprendió el lazo
de la asta, crugió por el aire un áspero zumbido y
al mismo tiempo se vió rodar desde lo alto de una
horqueta del corral, como si un golpe de lacha

[hacha] la hubiese dividido á cercen una cabeza
de niño cuyo tronco permaneció inmóvil sobre
su caballo de palo, lanzando por cada arteria un
largo chorro de sangre.

–Se cortó el lazo, gritaron unos: allá vá el toro.
Pero otros deslumbrados y atónitos guardaron
silencio porque todo fué como un relámpago.

Desparramóse un tanto el grupo de la puerta.
Una parte se agolpó sobre la cabeza y el cadáver
palpitante del muchacho degollado por el lazo,
manifestando horror en su atónito semblante, y
la otra parte compuesta de ginetes que no vieron
la catástrofe se escurrió en distintas direcciones en
pos del toro, vociferando y gritando: Allá va el
toro! Atajen! Guarda!–Enlaza, Siete pelos–Que te
agarra, Botija!–Va furioso; no se le pongan delante–
Ataja, ataja morado!–Dele espuela al mancarron–Ya
se metió en la calle sola.–Que lo ataje el diablo!

El tropel y voceria era infernal. Unas cuantas
negras achuradoras sentadas en hilera al borde del
zanjon oyendo el tumulto se acojieron y agaza-
paron entre las panzas y tripas que desenredaban y
devanaban con la paciencia de Penelope, lo que sin
duda las salvó por que el animal lanzó al mirarlos
un bufido aterrador, dió un brinco sesgado y siguió
adelante perseguido por los ginetes. Cuentan que
una de ellas se fué de cámaras; otra rezó diez salves

en dos minutos, y dos prometieron á San Benito no volver jamás á aquellos malditos corrales y abandonar el oficio de achuradoras. No se sabe si cumplieron la promesa.

El toro entre tanto tomó hácia la ciudad por una larga y angosta calle que parte de la punta mas aguda del rectángulo anteriormente descripto, calle encerrada por una zanja y un cerco de tunas, que llaman *sola* por no tener mas de dos casas laterales y en cuyo aposado centro habia un profundo pantano que tomaba de zanja á zanja. Cierto inglés, de vuelta de su saladero vadeaba este pantano á la sazon, paso á paso en un caballo algo arisco, y sin duda iba tan absorto en sus cálculos que no oyó el tropel de ginetes ni la griteria sino cuando el toro arremetia al pantano. Azorose de repente su caballo dando un brinco al sesgo y echó á correr dejando al pobre hombre hundido media vara en el fango. Este accidente, sin embargo, no detuvo ni refrenó la carrera de los perseguidores del toro, antes al contrario, soltando carcajadas sarcásticas-se amoló el gringo; levántate, gringo-esclamaron, y cruzando el pantano amasando con barro bajo las patas de sus caballos, su miserable cuerpo. Salió el gringo, como pudo, despues á la orilla, mas con la apariencia de un demonio tostado por las llamas del infierno que de un hombre blanco

pelirubio. Mas adelante al grito de al toro! al toro!
cuatro negras achuradores que se retiraban con su
presa se zabulleron en la zanja llena de agua, único
refugio que les quedaba.

El animal, entre tanto, despues de haber corrido
unas 20 cuadras en distintas direcciones asorando
con su presencia á todo viviente se metió por la
tranquera de una quinta donde halló su perdicion.
Aunque cansado, manifestaba brios y colérico
ceño; pero rodeábalo una zanja profunda y un
tupido cerco de pitas, y no habia escape. Juntáronse
luego sus perseguidores que se hallaban desvandados
y resolvieron llevarlo en un señuelo de bueyes para
que espiase su atentado en el lugar mismo donde
lo habia cometido.

Una hora despues de su fuga el toro estaba otra
vez en el Matadero donde la poca chusma que
habia quedado no hablaba sino de sus fechorias.
La aventura del gringo en el pantano exitaba
principalmente la risa y el sarcasmo. Del niño degollado por el lazo no quedaba sino un charco de
sangre: su cadáver estaba en el cementerio.

Enlazaron muy luego por las astas al animal que
brincaba haciendo hincapié y lanzando roncos
bramidos. Echáronle, uno, dos, tres piales; pero
infructuosos: al cuarto quedó prendido de una
pata: su brio y su furia redoblaron; su lengua

estirándose convulsiva arrojaba espuma, su nariz humo, sus ojos miradas encendidas–Desgarreten ese animal! esclamó una voz imperiosa. Matasiete se tiró al punto del caballo, cortóle el garron de una cuchillada y gambeteando en torno de él con su enorme daga en mano, se la hundió al cabo hasta el puño en la garganta mostrándola en seguida humeante y roja á los espectadores. Brotó un torrente de la herida, exhaló algunos bramidos roncos, vaciló y cayó el soberbio animal entre los gritos de la chusma que proclamaba á Matasiete vencedor y le adjudicaba en premio el matambre. Matasiete estendió, como orgulloso, por segunda vez el brazo y el cuchillo ensangrentado y se agachó á desollarle con otros compañeros.

Faltaba que resolver la duda sobre los órganos genitales del muerto clasificado provisoriamente de toro por su indomable fiereza; pero estaban todos tan fatigados de la larga tarea que la echaron por lo pronto en olvido. Mas de repente una voz ruda esclamó: aquí están los huevos, sacando de la barrija del animal y mostrando á los espectadores dos enormes testículos, signo inequívoco de su dignidad de toro. La risa y la charla fué grande; todos los incidentes desgraciados pudieron fácilmente esplicarse. Un toro en el Matadero era cosa muy rara, y aun vedada. Aquel, segun reglas de buena policia debió arrojarse á los perros; pero habia tanta escasez de carne y tantos hambrientos en la poblacion, que el señor Juez tuvo á bien hacer ojo lerdo.

En dos por tres estuvo desollado, descuartizado y colgado en la carreta el maldito toro. Matasiete colocó el matambre bajo el pellon de su recado y se preparaba á partir. La matanza estaba concluida á las 12, y la poca chusma que habia presenciado hasta el fin, se retiraba en grupos de á pié y de á caballo, ó tirando á la cincha algunas carretas cargadas de carne.

Mas de repente la ronca voz de un carnicero gritó–Allí viene un unitario! y al oir tan significativa palabra toda aquella chusma se detuvo como herida de una impresion subitanea.

–No le ven la patilla en forma de U? No traé divisa en el fraque ni luto en el sombrero.

–Perro unitario.

–Es un cajetilla.

–Monta en silla como los gringos.

–La mazorca con él.

–La tijera!

–Es preciso sobarlo.

–Trae pistoleras por pintar.

–Todos estos cajetillas unitarios son pintores como el diablo.

–A que no te le animas, Matasiete?

–A que nó?

–A que sí.

Matasiete era hombre de pocas palabras y de mucha accion. Tratándose de violencia, de agilidad, de destreza en el hacha, el cuchillo ó el caballo, no hablaba y obraba. Lo habian picado: prendió la espuela á su caballo y se lanzó á brida suelta al encuentro del unitario.

Era este un jóven como de 25 años de gallarda y bien apuesta persona que mientras salian en borboton de aquellas desaforadas bocas las anteriores esclamaciones trotaba hácia Barracas, muy ageno de temer peligro alguno. Notando empero, las significativas miradas de aquel grupo de dogos de matadero, echa maquinalmente la diestra sobre las pistoleras de su silla inglesa, cuando una pechada al sesgo del caballo de Matasiete lo arroja de los lomos del suyo tendiéndolo á la distancia boca arriba y sin movimiento alguno.

–Viva Matasiete! esclamó toda aquella chusma cayendo en tropel sobre la víctima como los caranchos rapaces sobre la osamenta de un buey devorado por el tigre.

Atolondrado todavia el jóven fué, lanzando una mirada de fuego sobre aquellos hombres feroces, hácia su caballo que permanecia inmóvil no muy distante á buscar en sus pistolas el desagravio y la venganza. Matasiete dando un salto le salió al encuentro y con fornido brazo asiéndolo de la corbata lo tendió en el suelo tirando al mismo tiempo la daga de la cintura y llevándola á su garganta.

Una tremenda carcajada y un nuevo viva estertorio volvió á victoriarlo.

Qué nobleza de alma! Qué bravura en los federales! siempre en pandilla cayendo como buitres sobre la víctima inerte.

–Deguéllalo, Matasiete–quiso sacar las pistolas. Deguéllalo como al Toro.

–Pícaro unitario. Es preciso tusarlo.

–Tiene buen pescuezo para el violin.

–Tocale el violin.

–Mejor es resbalosa.

–Probemos, dijo Matasiete y empezó sonriendo á pasar el filo de su daga por la garganta del caido, mientras con la rodilla izquierda le comprimia el pecho y con la siniestra mano le sujetaba por los cabellos.

–No, no le degüellen, esclamó de lejos la voz imponente del Juez del Matadero que se acercaba á caballo.

–A la casilla con él, á la casilla. Preparen la mashorca y las tijeras. Mueran los salvajes unitarios–Viva el Restaurador de las leyes!

–Viva Matasiete.

Mueran! Vivan! repitieron en coro los espectadores y atándole codo con codo, entre moquetes y tirones, entre vociferaciones é injurias arrastraron al infeliz jóven al banco del tormento como los sayones al Cristo.

La sala de la casilla tenia en su centro una grande y fornida mesa de la cual no salian los vasos de bebida y los naipes sino para dar lugar á las ejecuciones y torturas de los sayones federales del Matadero. Notábase ademas en un rincon otra mesa chica con recado de escribir y un cuaderno de apuntes y porcion de sillas entre las que resaltaba un sillon de brazos destinado para el Juez. Un hombre, soldado en apariencia, sentado en una de ellas cantaba al son de la guitarra la resbalosa, tonada de inmensa popularidad entre los federales, cuando la chusma llegando en tropel al corredor de la casilla lanzó á empellones al jóven unitario hácia el centro de la sala.

–A tí te toca la resbalosa, gritó uno.

–Encomienda tu alma al diablo.

–Está furioso como toro montaraz.

–Ya le amansará el palo.

–Es preciso sobarlo.

–Por ahora verga y tijera.

–Si no, la vela.

–Mejor será la mazorca.

–Silencio y sentarse, esclamó el Juez dejándose caer sobre su sillon. Todos obedecieron, mientras el jóven de pié encarando al Juez esclamó con voz preñada de indignacion.

–Infames sayones, que intentan hacer de mí?

–Calma! dijo sonriendo el juez; no hay que encolerizarse. Ya lo verás.

El jóven, en efecto, estaba fuera de sí de cólera. Todo su cuerpo parecia estar en convulsion: Su pálido y amoratado rostro, su voz, su lábio trémulo, mostraban el movimiento convulsivo de su corazon, la agitacion de sus nervios. Sus ojos de fuego parecian salirse de la órbita, su negro y lácio cabello se levantaba herizado. Su cuello desnudo y la pechera de su camisa dejaban entrever el latido violento de sus arterias y la respiracion anhelante de sus pulmones.

–Tiemblas? le dijo el Juez.

–De rabia, por que no puedo sofocarte entre mis brazos.

–Tendrias fuerza y valor para eso?

–Tengo de sobra voluntad y coraje para tí, infame.

–A ver las tijeras de tusar mi caballo–túsenlo á la federala.

Dos hombres le asieron, uno de la ligadura del

brazo, otro de la cabeza y en un minuto cortáronle la patilla que poblaba toda su barba por bajo, con risa estrepitosa de sus espectadores.

–A ver, dijo el Juez un vaso de agua para que se refresque.

–Uno de hiel te haria yo beber, infame.

Un negro petizo púsosele al punto delante con un vaso de agua en la mano. Dióle el jóven un puntapié en el brazo y el vaso fué á estrellarse en el techo salpicando el asombrado rostro de los espectadores.

–Este es incorrejible.

–Ya lo domaremos.

–Silencio, dijo el Juez, ya estás afeitado á la federala solo te falta el bigote. Cuidado con olvidarlo. Ahora vamos á cuentas.

–Por qué no traes divisa?

–Por que no quiero.

–No sabes que lo manda el Restaurador.

–La librea es para vosotros, esclavos, no para los hombres libres.

–A los libres se les hace llevar á la fuerza.

–Sí, la fuerza y la violencia bestial. Esas son vuestras armas; infames. El lobo, el tigre, la pantera tambien son fuertes como vosotros. Deberiais andar como ellas [ellos] en cuatro patas.

–No temes que el tigre te despedace?

–Lo prefiero á que maniatado me arranquen como el cuervo, una á una las entrañas.

–Por qué no llevas luto en el sombrero por la heroina?

–Porque lo llevo en el corazon por la Patria, por la Patria que vosotros habeis asesinado, infames!

–No sabes que así lo dispuso el Restaurador.

–Lo dispusisteis vosotros, esclavos, para lisonjear el orgullo de vuestro señor y tributarle vasallaje infame.

–Insolente! te has embravecido mucho. Te haré cortar la lengua si chistas.

–Abajo los calzones á ese mentecato cajetilla y á nalga pelada denle berga, bien atado sobre la mesa.

Apenas articuló esto el Juez cuatro sayones salpicados de sangre, suspendieron al jóven y lo tendieron largo á largo sobre la mesa comprimiéndole todos sus miembros.

–Primero degollarme que desnudarme; infame canalla.

Atáronle un pañuelo por la boca y empezaron á tironear sus vestidos. Encojíase el jóven, pateaba, hacia rechinar los dientes. Tomaban ora sus miembros la flexibilidad del junco, ora la dureza del fierro y su espina dorsal era el eje de un movimiento parecido al de la serpiente. Gotas de sudor fluian por su rostro grandes como perlas;

echaban fuego sus púpilas, su boca espuma, y las venas de su cuello y frente negreaban en relieve sobre su blanco cutis como si estuvieran repletas de sangre.

–Atenlo primero, esclamó el Juez.

–Está rujiendo de rabia, articuló un sayon.

En un momento liaron sus piernas en ángulo á los cuatro pies de la mesa volcando su cuerpo boca abajo. Era preciso hacer igual operacion con las manos, para lo cual soltaron las ataduras que las comprimian en la espalda. Sintiéndolas libres el jóven, por un movimiento brusco en el cual pareció agotarse toda su fuerza y vitalidad, se incorporó primero sobre sus brazos, despues sobre sus rodillas y se desplomó al momento murmurando – primero degollarme que desnudarme infame, canalla.

Sus fuerzas se habian agotado–inmediatamente quedó atado en cruz y empezaron la obra de desnudarlo. Entonces un torrente de sangre brotó borbolloneando de la boca y las narices del jóven y estendiéndose empezó á caer á chorros por entrambos lados de la mesa. Los sayones quedaron inmóbles y los espectadores estupefactos.

–Reventó de rabia el salvaje unitario, dijo uno.

–Tenia un rio de sangre en las venas articuló otro.

–Pobre diablo: queríamos únicamente divertirnos con él y tomó la cosa demasiado á lo serio, esclamó el juez frunciendo el ceño de tigre. Es preciso dar parte, desátenlo y vamos.

Verificaron la órden; echaron llave á la puerta y en un momento se escurrió la chusma en pos del caballo del Juez cabizbajo y taciturno.

Los federales habian dado fin á una de sus innumerables proesas.

En aquel tiempo los carniceros degolladores del Matadero eran los apóstoles que propagaban á verga y puñal la federacion rosina, y no es dificil imaginarse qué federacion saldria de sus cabezas y cuchillas. Llamaban ellos salvaje unitario, conforme á la jerga inventada por el Restaurador, patron de la cofradia, á todo el que no era degollador, carnicero, ni salvage, ni ladron; á todo hombre decente y de corazon bien puesto, á todo patriota ilustrado amigo de las luces y de la libertad; y por el suceso anterior puede verse á las claras que el foco de la federacion estaba en el Matadero.

APPENDIXES

I

Foreword to the 1871 Edition
by Juan María Gutiérrez

Originally published as a preface to the first printing of 'El matadero', in the *Revista del Río de la Plata*, Vol. I, No. 4, pp. 556–62, Buenos Aires, 1871; and later, slightly revised, as a footnote (pp. 209–14), when the story was collected in Vol. V of the *Obras completas de D. Esteban Echeverría*, Buenos Aires, Carlos Casavalle Editor, 1874.

An artist contributes to the study of society when he sets down on his canvas a typical scene that takes us back to the time and place it occurred and makes us believe we are there, living alongside his characters. But this is a rare achievement, and the few examples of it that exist are treasured like jewels not only for their artistic merits but also for the way of life they portray, a full understanding of which is the essence of history.

We Argentines, growing in age as a people and

progressing culturally as a society, are increasingly eager to find out about our past and to collect evidence from it to guide us in our judgements. But it is no easier to fulfil such a desire today than it was in antiquity. Since Argentina has had no national literature or art to make a record of its social types, these have come and gone as fleetingly as time itself.

Despite his rich imagination, Walter Scott would have been powerless to interest his contemporaries in picturesque medieval scenes had the manners and customs that make up the themes, action, and colour of his famous novels not already existed in chronicles or been depicted in paintings or carved in stone. Just as a ruin cannot be restored when all we know is its location, similarly, to comprehend a past time without actual evidence of it is a feat beyond human intelligence. Therefore, whenever we are fortunate enough to meet someone who bore witness to a bygone period in our lives, we should hasten to record that priceless evidence, thereby illuminating a hitherto blank page of our history.

Such is the case with the piece of writing published here. Its author's name alone is a recommendation, since his personal qualities are as familiar to us as his literary achievement. That this work was not meant to be published exactly as it left his pen is clear from the haste and raw realism with which it was written. The manuscript was jotted down so quickly that it cannot have taken longer to write than a typist would have needed to record it from dictation. We might envisage the writer as an artist opening his sketchbook to transcribe there in broad, rapid strokes the street scene before him, in order later – in the quiet of his studio – to create a picture of everyday life.

These drafts or sketches, or call them what you will, are of great value to connoisseurs of art, for they are spontaneous improvisations that allow the demeanour, the genius, and even the soul of the person who produced them to shine through with honesty. However rough a sketch may be, it reveals a personality, a character, and is therefore highly prized by anyone who loves what is original and truthful. At the same time, drafts of this kind are better than any other criteria on which to judge an artist's merits.

Apart from their historic value, which we shall point out in due course, the considerations just mentioned give this work an added significance. They allow us a further opportunity to under-stand the author of poems such as 'La cautiva' and 'El ángel caído' and to share the secret of how he composed or, as he said, 'crafted' his poetry. Those acquainted with this secret, which the poet himself would not have been able to explain even had he tried, know that his work is the result of deep reflection, of drafts begun and abandoned, of deliberation on society and the individual, of lengthy probing of his own conscience, of patient inquiry into events that he had not personally witnessed. When his palette was brimming with colours to match his ideas, which by then were sharp and clear in his mind, he plunged into his work with all the fire of a man inspired. In a short burst he would dash off fragments of his vast visionary ideas.

As a friend of the illustrious poet and editor of his collected works, I have studied the great number of manuscript pages and rough drafts that he left in considerable disarray, and I can provide documentary evidence of what I have said. His Don Juan figure was recreated several times over under various names, and the final version of the poem of which this character is the hero is the result of many drafts, all of which, when they lacked the sharpness and perfection Echeverría demanded of his work, he consigned to his desk drawer.

I found an interesting series of studies in epistolary form of the natural history, landscape, and inhabitants of the Argentine plains later used by the author in 'La cautiva'. The sense of solemn melancholy evoked by the poem is owed to the carefully observed setting in which the hapless characters of this drama of the wilderness move.

It was for a purpose that becomes clear in his poem 'Avellaneda' that the author drew the picture presented here in 'The Slaughteryard'. Chance and adversity brought Echeverría into contact with that quintessential part of Buenos Aires, the place where cattle are butchered for the city markets, and, just as a pathologist controls his feelings upon confronting a corpse, so too did the author when he stopped to watch the activity unfolding there and had the courage to write down what he saw in order one day to present it in all its ugliness to arbiters of social reform. With first-hand knowledge of the cast of mind and behaviour of the kind of men whom the tyrant chose as instruments of his system of government, Echeverría was able to depict with a masterly hand the sinister characters who bring about the downfall of the noble victim of the above-mentioned poem.

The notorious organization known as the Mazorca is to this day a matter of question, and people still ask who its members were and where with its weapons of terror and death it sprang from. The tale that follows will provide the answers. The proving ground, the cradle and school of these knife-wielding gendarmes, who sowed fear and mourning wherever the law was arbitrarily enforced, was the slaughteryard.

The poet was not without anxiety when he wrote this eloquent page in the struggle against tyranny. If the work had fallen into Rosas' hands, its author would have disappeared on the spot. He was well aware of the risk he was running; but the shakiness one notices in the handwriting, which is barely legible in the original manuscript, may be the result of rage rather than fear. His indignation appears in the form of irony. In one stroke, he lays bare the links between idolatry and fanaticism, opening his piece with Lenten practices that, in an inevitable extension of the events themselves, gradually degenerate into sanctioned murder, which is what happens when political fanaticism is injected into superstitious minds.

The scene is painted in strong reds, but this is not an exaggeration. Only such colours adequately depict the blood, the struggle with the ferocious bull, the cheek-by-jowl squabbling and the naked blade, the howling of the half-starved dogs, the flocks of scavenging birds, the noisy groups of ragged black women, and the bustle and clamour of the foul-mouthed butchers. The vivid colours of this picture are not toned down even by the arrival of the young man, who seems a victim of his own self-respect and background. Far from being intimidated and blenching before his torturers, he displays all the energy, moral integrity, and physical courage that offended honour arouses in a brave man.

The episode of the 'barbarous Unitarian' in the hands of the slaughteryard judge and his hench-men is not an invention but an actual incident such as happened more than once during that unhappy period. The only thing in this picture that might have sprung from the author's imagination is his moral awareness of what took place and the behaviour and the words of the victim, who conducts himself as the noble poet would have done in similar circumstances.

This valuable sketch would seem bland if, through an exaggerated respect for delicacy, the coarse words and phrases uttered by the characters in the tragedy were suppressed. Such language stands in no danger of being aped; on the contrary, linked by the author's skill to those who use it, these words are even farther removed from cultured usage and therefore for ever beyond the pale.

I have no idea why there has been a reluctance to record for posterity the characteristics of the Rosas dictatorship, when Argentina suffered a veritable period of terrorism that sent shock and horror throughout Europe and the Americas. Yet had I to produce written evidence and substantiation of the deeds that are the hallmark of that period, despite having heard them daily from the mouths of eye-witnesses, I would be hard put to it to find precise documentation. When these witnesses are dead, we shall find that everyone believes we were the victims not of a ruthless barbarian but of a bad dream that overcame us as we drowsed off one summer's afternoon.

A country that, for whatever reason, appears indifferent to its history and allows much of it to drift into oblivion is doomed to remain without a face of its own and to seem to the world insipid and bloodless. And if this failure to fulfil an obligation is the deliberate result of misconceived patriotism, which silences mistakes and crimes, then the omission is all the more deplorable. To serve a country's honour in such a way is no virtue but a crime dearly paid for, since it renders history useless either as an example or as a basis for reform.

Echeverría did not think in this fashion. He believed that a man cannot with his hand blot out the sun from anyone but himself, that the silence of eyewitnesses only stifles history, and that since we are obliged to speak out we must tell the truth. The author's tale is a page of history, a record of customs and scenes from everyday life, and a protest that does honour to all Argentines.

2

The South Matadero,
One of the Public Butcheries of Buenos Ayres
by Emeric Essex Vidal

Vidal (1791–1861), a Royal Navy purser and paymaster, served with a British detachment on the River Plate in the years 1817 and 1818. His aquatints, unlike previous pictorial material – mainly panoramas of the city viewed from the river – were the first to depict the streets and squares and marketplaces of Buenos Aires. The text printed below is from his book *Picturesque Illustrations of Buenos Ayres and Monte Video, consisting of Twenty-four Views: accompanied with descriptions of the scenery, and of the costumes, manners, &c. of the inhabitants of those cities and their environs*, London, 1820, pp. 35–40. The slaughteryard he records here in both prose and aquatint is not that of Echeverría's story, which was the city's south-west *matadero*, but a picture of the latter – 'The S.W. Matadero at Buenos Ayres (Killing Place)' – appears in another series of Vidal's work. The foregrounds of the two views are different, yet the skyline of church towers and domes in both were drawn from the same spot. Vidal's iribu is the black vulture (*Coragyps atratus*).

At Buenos Ayres there are four *Mataderos*, or public butcheries, one at each end, and two on the quarters of the city.

The view is taken from the south, and looks over the centre of the city, the south end being concealed by the olive grove on the right. The contiguous suburb is rather picturesque, the *pateos* (courts) of the houses being filled with orange and lemon-trees, which appear above the walls; and small gardens, filled with those trees, figs and olives, give the place an air of cultivation, which is miserably reversed upon turning the face towards the plain at the distance of a league or two.

To a foreigner nothing can be more disgusting than the mode of supplying this place with beef. The animals are all killed in these Mataderos on the open ground, wet or dry, in summer covered with dust, and in winter with mud. Each Matadero has several *corals*, or pounds, belonging to the different butchers. Into these the beasts are driven from the country, and let out one by one, to be slaughtered, being lazoed as they come out, hamstrung, and then thrown on the ground, after which their throats are cut. In this manner the butchers slaughter as many oxen as they require, leaving the carcases on the ground till all are killed, when they commence the operation of flaying. When this is finished, the carcases are cut up on the skin, which is the only protection from the bare ground, not into quarters as with us, but with an axe, into longitudinal sections across the ribs on each side of the back bone, thus dividing the carcase into three long mangled pieces, which are hung up in the carts, and carried, exposed to dust and filth, to the beef-market within the Plaza.

All the offal is scattered over the ground, and as a high-road leads across each of the Mataderos, this would be an intolerable nuisance, especially in summer, were it not for the flocks of carrion-birds, which devour every thing, and pick all the bones that are left as clean as possible, in less than an hour after the departure of the carts. A few privileged hogs share with the carrion-birds what remains on the ground; and herds of swine are always kept close to the Mataderos, and fed intirely on the bullocks' heads and livers. Nothing can be more disgusting than the appearance of the corals where these beasts are kept; indeed so revolting is it, that all foreigners at this place become Jews, in so far at least as regards the abhorrence of swine's flesh.

As the mode of lazoing is exhibited in the sketch, some description of it may be expected. The word *lazo* signifies a noose; and it is literally a noose that is used on this occasion. The lazo is an inch rope made of platted strips of hide, kept supple with grease. To one extremity is attached a strong iron ring, through which the other end is passed, and fastened to the girth of the saddle. This rope, about twelve yards long, is held in coils in one hand, while the noose, lengthened to the convenience of the thrower, is in the other. On approaching the bullock, the noose is whirled round the head with a twist of the hand to prevent its entangling, and presently thrown, to its full extent, loose and round over the horns or any part that is desired, the thrower being so sure of his mark, that he will catch the animal by the horns, or any one of his legs, or his tail if he pleases. Great quickness of eye is required to draw the noose tight at the proper moment.

In this manner the wild cattle in the plains of the Pampas, and also those belonging to the *estantias* (grazing-farms), are caught and killed. Here the horses are so trained, that when the beast is once fast, the horse will keep the lazo tight, and prevent his running, while the rider dismounts and kills him. At the farms three persons are often engaged in this business. One of them rides in among the cattle, and selecting a beast, throws his lazo over the horns, and gallops away till the rope is run out. The second is then ready with his noose, and watching the opportunity of the beast kicking and struggling, he entangles one of the hind legs. Both the horses immediately draw the ropes tight in opposite directions, and hold them so firmly that the beast is unable to move. A third man then comes up, hamstrings the hind leg that is not secured, upon which the animal immediately falls, and his throat is cut. Though to a stranger this may appear a tedious process, it is performed by experienced persons in four or five minutes.

Another method of killing cattle in the public butcheries is this: A machine with a pulley and winch is erected at the extremity of the inclosure. The horns of a bullock are entangled in a rope attached to this machine, by which he is drawn forward till his head passes through an opening in the paling, where a man, provided with a strong dagger, stabs the beast between the horns in the pith of the neck, which occasions almost instantaneous death.

By means of the lazo they also catch horses, as well as those that run wild at the time. It is very rarely indeed that they miss their aim, though going at full speed; and a man, however cautious, can no more avoid being taken by the lazo, than the animals which they hunt. It is used by the straggling robbers, who sometimes infest the roads at a distance from towns. In an open country, the only resource which a man has in such a case is, to throw himself on the ground, keeping his legs and arms as close to it as possible, that no room may be left for the rope to get underneath them. Among trees or underwood, the noose is less dangerous; and by a rapid approach to the robber, before he has time to throw the lazo, his dexterity may also be foiled. This rope is so strong that, though not thicker than one's little finger, it will hold the wildest bull, when his efforts to escape would break a hempen rope of much larger dimensions.

The carrion-bird, which renders such important services by devouring the large quantities of offal and animal relics that would otherwise taint the atmosphere, is a species of gull, with yellow bill and feet, blue back and shoulders, and the rest of the body beautifully white. These birds not only frequent the butcheries of Monte Video and Buenos Ayres, but also the public places of those cities, picking up such offal as they can find. They are likewise seen in immense numbers on the beach, when the waves have cast upon it the carcase of a whale or other fish. Sometimes too they will leave the coast, and proceed so far as one hundred leagues into the interior, attracted by carcases and heaps of flesh, which are left to spoil in the fields and savannahs.

The *iribu*, or vulture, another carrion-bird, is very common in Paraguay, though it is not met with beyond the parallel of Buenos Ayres. It is known from tradition, that at the time of the conquest, and even long afterwards, this bird was not found at Monte Video, but that it followed vessels to that part of the country. It is asserted that it does not build a nest, but deposits two white eggs in holes in rocks or trees. M. de Azara informs us, that, for more than a year, he had opportunies of observing an iribu which was kept in a house: it was extremely tame, could distinguish its master, and would accompany him in excursions of eight or ten leagues, flying over his head, and sometimes settling on his carriage. It always came when called, and never joined others of its species to feed; neither would it eat but from the hand, nor touch any meat that was not cut into very small pieces. Another iribu, which was likewise tame, accompanied its master on journeys of more than a hundred leagues to Monte Video; but when it perceived that he was taking the road home, it would hasten before him, and thus announce to its mistress the return of her husband.

This bird passes the greatest part of the day upon trees or palisades, watching for some person to throw out fragments of meat, or to kill a sheep. In general, several of the iribus assemble on the same tree; and as they are never molested, they live every where in peace and security. If any noise or object frightens them when they are assembled upon carrion, they all at once set up a cry of *hu* in a nasal tone, and it is the only one they ever utter. Whether single or in company, they never attack or harass any animal; and when several of them fall upon a dead one of small size, each strives to tear off a piece as well as he can, without quarrelling with his companions. They begin by devouring the eyes, then the tongue, and such of the intestines as they can draw out. If the animal has a very strong hide, and a dog, or some other carnivorous beast, has not begun upon it, they leave it after they have plucked out the parts abovementioned; but if they find any opening, they devour all the flesh to the very bones, which they leave covered with the skin alone. They sometimes follow travellers and vessels, and live upon the offal and filth that are thrown away. When wounded, they cast up all that they have swallowed.

The head and neck of the iribu are bare and wrinkled; the whole of the plumage is black, excepting the quills of the first six wing-feathers, which are white: its total length is about two feet, including the tail, which measures from six to seven inches.

There is another species of bird in this country, which is not less greedy of carrion than the iribu. The *caracara* will not only fall upon dead carcases, but if he perceives a vulture about to swallow a piece of flesh, will follow him till he has dropped his repast. Four or five of these birds will sometimes join in the pursuit of prey, and it is generally believed, that in this manner they will kill ostriches and fawns. In sheepfolds that are not guarded by a dog, a single caracara will devour the umbilical cord and tear out the intestines of the newly dropped lambs.

3

Accounts by Other Travellers,
1818–63

a.

Major Alexander Gillespie landed in Argentina in 1807 as an officer in the British army that seized and occupied Buenos Aires in an unauthorized operation that became known to the Argentines as 'the second English invasion'. Taken prisoner and sent to live in internment on the outskirts of the city, Gillespie described himself as 'Alternately a conqueror and a captive upon the shores of La Plata'. His memoirs, *Gleanings and Remarks: collected during many months of residence at Buenos Ayres, and within the Upper Country*, printed for him in Leeds, in 1818, deal with events of the years 1806–7. The following description (pp. 77–8) of the slaughtering at a *saladero*, or meat-salting establishment, is one of the earliest on record. The first *saladero* in the Argentine was located at Quilmes, in 1795. As a monopoly of rich landowners of the Province of Buenos Aires, meat-salting became intimately connected with Rosas and his Federalist policies.

[A] simple improvement in grain and feeding, would yield an immense profit to the adventurer, and in a short space would stamp a high character upon their exports of beef, which is one of the most important staples of this part of South America. From the manner, and the temper of blood in which the animal has been hitherto butchered, it could not be expected that its meat was calculated for cure. The ox marked out, has been pursued at full speed until lassoed by the horseman, another in the chase does the same, and both striking off at opposite angles, either threw him down, or retarded his progress, while a third dismounting, hamstringed him in both hinder legs, and then cut his throat. In this state of fever was he killed, skinned, and after an inadequate bleeding, the flakes of flesh were torn off, put into a barrel of brine, during twenty-four hours, dried in the sun after being drained, and packed up for use or traffic. Owing to the green food, and no sugar being mixed with the preparation, the meat became hard, and sometimes putrid; in which state it will never repay except in the West Indies, where it is readily bought up for the negroes, who have generally a strong predilection for food very salt, and even tainted.

b.

Francis Bond Head (1793–1879), a former captain in the Royal Engineers, arrived in Buenos Aires in July 1825, to supervise an English mining operation in the Andes. The *matadero* described in his vivid *Rough Notes Taken During Some Rapid Journeys Across the Pampas and Among the Andes*, London, 1826, (pp. 33–5), was the city's northern slaughteryard, on the road leading to the Recoleta cemetery.

During the short time I was at Buenos Aires, I lived in a house out of the town, which was opposite the English burying-ground, and very near the place where the cattle were killed. This latter spot was about four or five acres, and was altogether devoid of pasture; at one end of it there was a large corral enclosed by rough stakes, and divided into a number of pens, each of which had a separate gate. These *cells* were always full of cattle doomed for slaughter. I several times had occasion to ride over this field, and it was curious to see its different appearances. In passing it in the day or evening, no human being was to be seen: the cattle up to their knees in mud, and with nothing to eat, were standing in the sun, occasionally lowing, or rather roaring to each other. The ground in every direction was covered with groups of large white gulls, some of which were earnestly pecking at the slops of blood which they had surrounded, while others were standing upon their tip-toes, and flapping their wings as if to recover their appetite. Each slop of blood was the spot where a bullock had died; it was all that was left of his history, and pigs and gulls were rapidly consuming it. Early in the morning no blood was to be seen; a number of horses, with the lassos hanging to their saddles, were standing in groups apparently asleep: the mataderos were either sitting or lying on the ground close to the stakes of the corral, and smoking segars; while the cattle, without metaphor, were waiting until the last hour of their existence should strike; for as soon as the clock of the Recolata struck, the men all vaulted on their horses, the gates of all the cells were opened, and in a very few seconds, there was a scene of apparent confusion which it is quite impossible to describe. Every man had a wild bullock at the end of his lasso; some of these animals were running away from the horses, and some were running at them; many were roaring, some were hamstrung, and running about on their stumps; some were killed and skinned, while occasionally one would break the lasso. The horse would often fall upon his rider, and the bullock endeavor to regain his liberty, until the horsemen at full speed caught him with the lasso, tripping him off the ground in a manner that might apparently break every bone in his body. I was more than once in the middle of this odd scene, and was really sometimes obliged to gallop for my life, without exactly knowing where to go, for it was often Scylla and Charybdis.

c.

Charles Darwin first set eyes on the River Plate sometime in July 1832. From then until 10 June 1834, when *H.M.S. Beagle* 'bade farewell for ever to Tierra del Fuego', he recorded some of the most memorable and valuable pictures of the Argentine ever penned. The following is part of the 20 September 1833 entry from his *Journal and Remarks. 1832–1836.*, published in 1839 and later more commonly known as the *Voyage of the* Beagle.

The great *corral* where the animals are kept for slaughter to supply food to this beef-eating population, is one of the spectacles best worth seeing. The strength of the horse as compared to that of the bullock is quite astonishing: a man on horseback having thrown his lazo round the horns of a beast, can drag it any where he chooses. The animal having ploughed up the ground with out-stretched legs, in vain efforts to resist the force, generally dashes at full speed to one side; but the horse immediately turning to receive the shock, stands so firmly, that the bullock is almost thrown down, and one would think, would certainly have its neck dislocated. The struggle is not, however, one of fair strength; the horse's girth being matched against the bullock's extended neck. In a similar manner a man can hold the wildest horse, if caught with the lazo, just behind the ears. When the bullock has been dragged to the spot where it is to be slaughtered, the *matador* with great caution cuts the hamstrings. Then is given the death bellow; a noise more expressive of fierce agony than any I know: I have often distinguished it from a long distance, and have always known that the struggle was then drawing to a close. The whole sight is horrible and revolting, the ground is almost made of bones; and the horses, and riders are drenched with gore.

d.

Robert Elwes left 'a record of travels, undertaken for no purpose but my own amusement' in his book *A Sketcher's*

Tour Round the World, London, 1854, two chapters of which are devoted to Uruguay and the Argentine. This picture (pp. 112–14) is of the Barracas meat-salting factories near the mouth of the Riachuelo, in the southern port area of Buenos Aires. The blockade referred to in the last sentence is that of Anglo-French forces during the years 1845–7.

Hides, tallow, and jerked beef are the chief exports of Buenos Ayres; and the quantity of cattle driven in from the country and slaughtered, is enormous. Near the town are large killing and salting establishments, called Saladeras, the principal at Barraca, where a creek runs up from the river, affording great facilities for shipping. The saladeras here, five or six in number, are on so large a scale that when in full work (which is not all the year), nearly five hundred head of cattle a day are killed at each. The rapidity with which they are killed and cut up is wonderful. Several corrals full of cattle surround the yard, and from these about sixty beasts are driven into a small enclosure, which terminates with a sliding door, raised above a platform on wheels. A block is fixed over the doorway, and through this is passed a lasso, the end of which is made fast to a couple of horses, each having a rider. The butcher then stands on a board running round the outside of the enclosure, near the top of the rails, and throws the noose of the lasso over the head of one of the bullocks, when the horsemen gallop off, dragging the entangled animal up to the block; and one thrust of the knife piercing him just where the head joins the neck, he falls dead on the platform, and is drawn away. In this manner a whole herd are quickly dispatched.

The dead bullock is pushed under a long shed, where about a dozen men, covered with filth and dust are each busy on a carcase. The flesh is cut off in flakes, the bones disjointed, and the skin taken off at the same time. I looked on at one fellow dressed in a poncho; and thought that, by the rapidity and sureness with which he handled his long knife, he must have been at this work from a child. At last he looked up, and said to me in a rich brogue: "Is it the first time yer honour has seen this sort of business?" He was one of the numerous Irishmen who have emigrated to this country. The flakes of meat are put by to make jerked beef, so called from the native name "charqui," the joints and other parts are thrown into huge coppers and boiled down for tallow; and the heads are ranged in order by themselves. After the horns are taken off, the front of the skulls with the bone of the horns, are used to build walls round the saladeras, and have a most curious appearance. Sometimes the roads are repaired with them, and very unsightly they make them look. As may be supposed, the smell from these saladeras is dreadful; and the first time I rode down to the Barraca, I was nearly sick, though I soon became accustomed to it. In the evening, the stench is often very strong in the city, as on every side there is beef, beef, beef. The pigs eat beef (but more frequently horse-flesh); the poultry eat it, and it is said that it may be tasted in their eggs; the ducks are fed on beef, and even in the pigeon-house a large lump is thrown for the pigeons to peck at. Fleas and flies swarm everywhere, fostered, I suppose by the quantity of cattle and beef. All sorts of animal food are plentiful; and when the English fleet blockaded Buenos Ayres, instead of there being any scarcity in the town, it cheapened everything to a wonderful degree, as the country had no sale for its produce.

e.

In 1861, Thomas Woodbine Hinchliff spent several months roaming Brazil and, more extensively, the republics of the River Plate. In Buenos Aires, he stayed at the suburban country house of his cousin, Woodbine Parish, the English

Consul. The following extracts are from Hinchliff's *South American Sketches*, London, 1863, pp. 67–73.

A few days after my arrival in Buenos Ayres, I was taken by a friend to see some of the *Saladeros* and the *Barracas* a little beyond the southern extremities of the city. The saladeros are enormous establishments in which cattle are slaughtered for their hides and tallow, and their flesh converted into jerked beef: the barracas are store-houses for produce. On approaching this district there were plenty of indications of the trade in dead beasts. In one place was a vast heap of what I at first imagined must be gigantic mussel-shells, but they soon proved to be hoofs: a little farther the land was protected from the encroachments of the Riachuelo river by a wall composed of thousands of skulls of cattle patched with sods of turf. Large and fierce dogs in great numbers lurked about in corners, licking their lips after some dainty bit of offal surreptitiously walked off with, and looking as if they would soon take to the legs of a visitor if their natural supplies were curtailed. Countless seagulls, surfeited with their filthy breakfast, were lazily trying to digest it on the land which they whitened with their presence, now and then whirling about for a few moments, as if shaking themselves to make room for a fresh supply of garbage. Presently we saw a mighty cloud of dust, whence came a sound like muffled thunder, mixed with screams and wild yells. Stand clear! get out of the way! here comes a drove of about a thousand cattle from the country to be slaughtered at the saladeros. Not with the decorous march at Smithfield come these devoted beasts – quite another style of thing, and well worth seeing.

Four or five *peons*, or drivers, in brilliant *ponchos* of red, blue, and yellow, ride in front at full gallop, cracking their whips, and screaming to one another while you gladly draw up near the wall to get out of the way as they charge towards you. Close at their heels comes the whole herd, heads down and tails up, going at their maddest speed, encouraged thereto by more peons at their sides. On they go, thundering through the cloud of dust, and at last the mad line is ended by another set of peons all shouting and urging on the wild race in such a state of whip-cracking excitement, that even a calm spectator feels the spell, and is almost ready to give up his soul to the possession of the galloping ghost of Mazeppa.

Half-stifled with dust, we went on our way to the saladeros, where we were to see the completion of bovine destiny, and arrived there about a quarter of an hour before the slaughter commenced. About 800 beasts had been driven into a *corral* or enclosure, made of strong posts nearly a foot thick, one side of which towards the yard tapered off into a kind of funnel about six feet wide, which was crossed by a strong bar with an iron pulley in it. This was approached by a small tramway, upon which travelled a truck large enough to carry two of the animals at the same time....

Two men seize on each, and cut their throats; the hide is taken off with inconceivable skill and rapidity; knives glance, and with light, but marvellously accurate touch, the head and limbs disappear. In about five minutes the animal has literally gone to pieces, vanished, almost before he has done kicking. The hide is hung up in one place; the legs are on different hooks; the good meat is hung in huge slabs to cool upon long railings; and the bony structure is carried off to the steaming vats. Meanwhile the fatal lazo is thrown again and again with horrible monotony, and the whole platform is covered with animals flying to pieces so quickly that you cannot follow the operation. In a moderate day's work the whole eight hundred will be disposed of in this way. I never saw so disgusting a sight, and could not help thinking as I watched these wild-looking men, how quickly they might have turned us into unrecognisable jerked beef and candles for exportation....

On the northern and southern sides of the city are the chief places for slaughtering animals to supply the inhabitants with food. A large piece of ground is surrounded by strong pens or enclosures, in which the cattle are shut up till a buyer comes. He comes, like all the rest of the South American world, on horseback, and selects his beast, which is then driven out into the open space: the mounted butchers pursue it at full speed; whizz goes the fatal lazo; the animal is instantly cut up where it happens to fall; and its mortal remains, disjointed in a way that would astonish a Briton, are carried away in a cart. The fowls of the air and the dogs of the field quarrel for the offal with herds of loathsome swine; and the horror which I conceived for pork brought up upon these independent principles was so great that I can hardly yet look upon English dairy-fed with anything like complacency. Little urchins resort to these places and practise upon the seagulls with the national weapon of the *bolas*, consisting of three balls connected by strings or strips of hide, which when whirled skillfully entangle the legs or wings of the beast or bird against which they are directed: and I have seen a couple of filthy negro-women squatting on the blood-soaked ground, and chattering like magpies over the disgusting operation of scraping every atom of grease from the intestines, which are left in all directions to the protection of Providence, and these loathsome harpies.

4
Wearing the Federalist Colour
by Robert Elwes

From *A Sketcher's Tour* (1854), pp. 115–16. The fact that an English traveller, his ear unaccustomed to the Spanish language, records that he heard the words *constitución* and *restorado* (they would have been *confederación* and *restaurador*) only attests to the essential accuracy of his observations.

I found Buenos Ayres a pleasant place to stay in. The chief amusement was riding; but there was a tolerable opera in the city, and an Italian company. It was well attended, few gentlemen appearing in the front row of the boxes. The ladies usually dress in white, but each had a little bow of red ribbon in their hair. This is the colour of Rosas, or rather the federal colour, and all were obliged to wear it. The ladies are generally handsome, of a very good style, and winning manners; and in few countries could you see so many pretty faces and such well-dressed women, as in the Opera House of Buenos Ayres. In the Pampas, and among the lower orders, on the contrary, though the men were often very handsome, I never saw one good-looking woman.

The gentlemen of Buenos Ayres were at this time all obliged to wear red waistcoats, as well as a red band round the hat, and a red ribbon in the button-hole. The red waistcoats at an evening party, or at the opera house, have a curious effect, and make the wearers look like a swarm of club footmen.

At the opera every night, just before the performances began, the curtain rose, and the principal actors were discovered standing on the stage, when one cried – "Viva la Confederacion Argentina!" and all the others answered, "Viva!" "Viva la Constitucion!" was then called out, with the same response, followed in succession by – "Viva el Restorado, Rosas!" "Mueran los salvajes Unitarios!" (Death to the savage Unitarians.) The curtain then fell, and again rising, the opera began. All the actors wore their bow of red ribbon, and when the part of a "gentleman" came on, he presented himself in a red waistcoat; and even Amina herself, in the "Sonnambula," was obliged to walk in her sleep with the red badge in her hair. The forbidden colours, denoting the Unitarian or opposition and Monte Videan party, are blue, green, and yellow, and these are never seen. Oddly enough, the Buenos Ayrean flag is blue, striped with white.

Foreigners were not obliged to wear either the waistcoat or the ribbon, but I wore the latter when crossing the Pampas. At this time Rosas had the people completely under his command, and they were forced to obey his most arbitrary mandates. On Sundays and fiesta days he generally exercised the National Guard; and as some citizens, who were not enrolled in its ranks, had laughed at their having to turn out for drill in the hot day, whilst others were amusing themselves, Rosas ordered that no one should stir from his house, or even look from his housetop or window, while the exercise was going on. At half-past three, therefore, when there was exercise, a gun was fired, and every one retired to his house and stayed there till another gun at sunset withdrew the interdict. During the interval, the police perambulated the streets, and only women and officers in uniform were allowed to pass.

5
Federalist Verses

The two pieces below, Federalist verses or songs, were produced as broadsides, or leaflets, for popular consumption during the Rosas era. Neither is signed or dated, but from internal evidence they appear to be from the year 1837.

The first, published by the Imprenta del Estado, the state printing office, is headed with the obligatory mantra upholding the Argentine Confederation and calling for the death of the savage, or barbarous, Unitarians:

¡VIVA LA CONFEDERACION ARGENTINA!
¡Mueran los salvajes Unitarios!

The second set of verses, produced by the Imprenta Argentina, bears only the first line of the mantra and no title. The text excoriates Andrés Santa Cruz, a former general in San Martín's Army of Independence and president of Bolivia, who, as head of a union of Bolivia and Peru during the years 1836 to 1839, was a threat to the integrity of Argentina's northern borders. Incensed as well by the protection that Santa Cruz afforded leading Unitarian exiles, Rosas was obliged in 1837 to send Alejandro Heredia into combat with the Bolivian leader. (The Blanco mentioned in the verses, line 33, is probably the Chilean Blanco Encalada, who also led an attack on Santa Cruz.) A special feature of the piece is the acrostic, in which the first letters of the lines spell out 'MUERA SANTA CRUZ POR VYL Y TRAIDOR POR UNITARYO IMPIO' – Death to Santa Cruz the Vile Traitor and Ungodly Unitarian. In the original of the broadside, the first letters of the acrostic are printed in bold face with the letters aligned so as to be read with the left-hand margin tilted to become the bottom of the page.

Both texts, taken from the photographic reproductions in Fermín Chávez's *Iconografía de Rosas y de la Federación; nuevos aportes*, Buenos Aires, 1972 – pp. 287 and 289, respectively – are given here in the style and spelling of the 1830s.

In the 'Cancion del Violin' Por un Federal Neto ('Song of the Violin' by a True Federalist), for the significance of the words *violín* and *violón* ('violin' and 'double bass') see the Glossary, p. 53.

a.

CANCION DEL VIOLIN,
Por un Federal Neto.

CORO.
Federales fieles
Al Restaurador,
Con los gambeteros
Violin y violon.

[CHORUS. *Federalists loyal to the Restorer, for the spineless a knife across the throat.*]

I
A los federales
De composicion,
Que con los salvajes
Forman reunion,
Verga por los lomos
Sin cuenta y razon;
Y si se resisten,
Violin y violon.

Coro, etc.

[For lukewarm Federalists who fraternize with the savages, a stick for their backs on principle;

and if they object, a knife across the throat. *Chorus, etc.*]

2
El que con salvajes
Tenga relacion,
La verga y degüello
Por esta traicion:
Que el santo sistema
De Federacion
Le dá á los salvajes
Violin y violon.

Coro, etc.

[For anyone having truck with the savages, the stick and a slit throat for their treachery; let the holy system of Federation give the savages a knife across the throat. *Chorus, etc.*]

3
Paz con los salvajes
No habrá nunca, no,
Mientras viva ROSAS
El Restaurador:
Así los esclavos
Del vil pardejon

Tendrán como su amo
Violin y violon.

Coro, etc.

[Peace with the savages will never ever be while
Rosas the Restorer is alive; and so the slaves of the
vile mongrel {Rosas' epithet for Fructuoso Rivera, an
Uruguayan caudillo who opposed him} will have as
their master a knife across the throat. *Chorus, etc.*]

4
Sigamos á ROSAS
El Restaurador
Fiel á los principios
Que nos enseñó;
Y á los enemigos
De nuestra nacion,
Démosle los netos
Violin y violon.

Coro, etc.

[Let us follow Rosas, the Restorer of the Laws,
loyal to the principles he instilled in us; and to the
nation's foes we'll mete out a pure knife across the
throat. *Chorus, etc.*]

b.

Mísero, vil y traidor,
Unitario, impío, ateo,
Eterno baldon tu oprobio
Raza inmunda del averno.
Al hondo abismo desciende
Súbito, monstruo funesto,
Al grito heróico que suena,
¿No escuchais el ronco éco?
¡Traidor! repite en las breñas,
10   Airado se irrita el viento,
Cóncavas las sierras se abren,
Retumban sus hondos senos;
Una hórrida tempestad
Zumba de Marte violento,
Palas fiera los caballos
Ostiga del carro horrendo,
Rápido, audaz, impetuoso,
Venganza y guerra encendiendo;
Y al esplendor de su antorcha
20   ¡Libertad! dicen los pueblos,
Y á dar muerte á Santa-Cruz,
Todos altivos marchemos.
Rotas ya están las cadenas
Al esforzado denuedo,

Inmortal, heróico, invicto,
De los patriotas que un tiempo,
Osaron romper el yugo
Regio y oprobioso ferreo?
¿Podrán permitir que aleves
30   ¡O cara patria! tus fueros,
Rompan inicuos traidores
Unitarios? ¡oh perversos!
¿No veis á Blanco y Heredia,
Invencibles con denuedo
Trepar escarpadas cumbres,
Al son del clarin guerrero;
Rasgando el velo ominoso
Y de valor dar ejemplo?
¡Oid, que muerte pronùncian
40   Irritados de ardor cruento!....
Mientras la Patria Argentina,
Prepara en su sacro templo,
Insignias á los campeones
Olivas á los Gobiernos?

[(1-22) Wretched, vile, traitorous, Unitarian, ungodly, atheist; eternal shame your infamy, foul race
from hell. Into the bottomless abyss you descend,
evil monster, on hearing the heroic cry that rings
forth. Can you not make out the harsh echo?
'Traitor!' it repeats in the scrubland; angry, it angers

the winds; the hollow sierras open, their deep breast thundering; violent Mars blows a monstrous storm; fierce Pallas whips the horses of her grim chariot – swift, bold, impetuous – kindling war and revenge. And to the splendour of her torch, the people cry 'Freedom!' Let us all march proudly, dealing death to Santa Cruz. (23–44) The chains are already shattered, through the brave spirit – immortal, heroic, invincible – of the patriots who once dared break Spain's shameful iron yoke. Shall it be permitted, O beloved Homeland, that wicked, traitorous Unitarians break your laws? Wretches! Do you not see Blanco and Heredia, invincible with resolution, scaling sheer peaks to the sound of martial trumpets, rending the ominous veil, and giving an example of valour? Hearken to the death they pledge, inflamed with merciless ardor. Meanwhile in its sacred temple the Argentine Nation prepares medals for the victors and olive branches for Governments!]

6
'La refalosa'
by Hilario Ascasubi

Hilario Ascasubi (1807–75) ranks as one of the most original and colourful figures in the annals of Argentine literature. He was a stripling sailor, a printer, an inveterate founder of periodicals, a soldier (at one time or another, he served under generals Paz, Lamadrid, Lavalle, and Urquiza), and a passionate advocate of the Unitarian cause. In 1831, after misadventures in the struggle against Rosas' dictatorship, Ascasubi went into in exile in Uruguay. Living there for the next twenty years, he endured the long blockade of Montevideo by local troops allied to the Federalists. Having set up a bakery, he made a large sum of money, part of which he used to support General Lavalle. At the battle of Caseros, in which Rosas met defeat, Ascasubi was an aide-de-camp of General Urquiza, whom he later turned against. A tireless entrepreneur, Ascasubi invested in civic improvements such as bringing gas to Buenos Aires and founding its celebrated opera house, the Teatro Colón.

His poems, which are in the tradition of River Plate gauchesco literature, document their particular era with anecdotal and topical material that is often written in a satirical burlesque style. He collected his works and published them in Paris, in 1872, in three large volumes (*Paulino Lucero, Aniceto el Gallo,* and *Santos Vega*). The text of 'La refalosa' printed here is taken from pp. 130–4 of the Paris edition of that first volume, whose full title, embracing two long subtitles, runs: *Paulino Lucero, or The Gauchos of the River Plate, singing and doing battle against the tyrants of the republics of Argentina and Uruguay (1839 to 1851), in which are recounted all the episodes of the nine-year siege heroically withstood by Montevideo as well as the campaigns waged elsewhere in Uruguay by gaucho patriots up to the overthrow of the tyrant Juan Manuel de Rosas and his allies.*

Ascasubi painstakingly annotated his pages with footnotes that explain a wealth of obscure words, slang terms, local expressions, and historical asides, thereby providing scholars and readers of nineteenth-century Argentine literature with an incomparable lexicon. In 'La refalosa', he glossed the following words: *maniador* (line 17); *sobeo* (line 23); and *vilote* (line 39).

LA REFALOSA

———

Amenaza de un mashorquero y degollador de los sitiadores de Montevideo dirigida al gaucho JACINTO CIELO, gacetero y soldao de la Legión Argentina, defensora de aquella plaza.

Mirá, Gaucho salvajon,
que no pierdo la esperanza,
y no es chanza,
de hacerte probar qué cosa
es *Tin tin* y *Refalosa*.
Ahora te diré cómo es:
escuchá y no te asustés;
que para ustedes es canto
mas triste que un Viernes Santo.

———

10 *Unitario* que agarramos
       lo estiramos;
ó paradito no más,
       por atrás,
lo amarran los compañeros
por supuesto, *mashoqueros*,

[143]

y ligao
con un *maniador* doblao,
ya queda codo con codo
y desnudito ante todo.
20   ¡Salvajon!
Aqu[i] empieza su aflicion.

Luego despues, á los *pieses*
un *sobeo* en tres dobleces
    se le atraca,
y queda como una estaca
lindamente asigurao,
    y parao
lo tenemos clamoriando;
y como medio chanciando
30   lo pinchamos,
y lo que grita, cantamos
la *refalosa* y *tin tin,*
    sin violin.

Pero seguimos el *son*
en la vaina del *laton,*
    que asentamos
el cuchillo, y le *tantiamos*
con las uñas el *cogote.*
¡Brinca el salvaje *vilote*
40   que da risa!

Cuando algunos en camisa
se empiezan á revolcar,
  y á llorar,
que es lo que mas nos divierte;
  de igual suerte
que al Presidente le agrada,
y larga la carcajada
  de alegría,
al oir la musiquería
50 y la broma que le damos
al salvaje que amarramos.

  Finalmente:
cuando creemos conveniente
despues que nos divertimos
grandemente, decidimos
  que al salvaje
el resuello se le ataje;
  y á derechas
lo agarra uno de las mechas,
60   mientras otro
lo sujeta como á potro
  de las patas,
que si se mueve es á gatas.

  Entre tanto,
nos clama por cuanto santo

tiene el cielo;
pero hay no mas por consuelo
á su queja:
abajito de la oreja,
70   con un puñal bien templao
y afilao,
que se llama el *quita penas,*
le atravesamos las venas
del pescuezo.
¿Y qué se le hace con eso?
larga sangre que es un gusto,
y del susto
entra á revolver los ojos.

¡Ah, hombres flojos!
80   hemos visto algunos de estos
que se muerden y hacen gestos,
y visajes
que se pelan los salvajes,
largando tamaña lengua;
y entre nosotros no es mengua
el besarlo,
para medio contentarlo.

¡Qué jarana!
nos reimos de buena gana
90   y muy mucho,

de ver que hasta les da chucho;
y entonces lo desatamos
    y soltamos;
y lo sabemos parar
para verlo REFALAR
    en la sangre!
hasta que le da un calambre
y se *cai* á patalear,
    y á temblar
100   muy fiero, hasta que se estira
el salvaje: y, lo que espira,
    le sacamos
una *lonja* que apreciamos
    el sobarla,
y de *manea* gastarla.

De ahi se le cortan orejas,
barba, patilla y cejas;
    y pelao
lo dejamos arrumbao,
110   para que engorde algun chancho,
    ó carancho.

  . . . .

Con que ya ves, Salvajon;
nadita te ha de pasar
despues de hacerte gritar:
¡Viva la Federacion!

[147]

[The Slippery Dance

[*The caveat of a Mazorca cut-throat laying siege to
Montevideo, addressed to the gaucho JACINTO
CIELO, a newspaper scribbler and soldier of the*
Argentine Legion, *defenders of that stronghold.*

[(1–9) See here, you Gaucho savage, I'm looking
forward – and this is no joke – to giving you a taste
of what *snick-snick* and the Slippery Dance are.
Let me describe them. Listen and don't be scared;
for you lot they're a music more melancholy than
Good Friday.

[(10–21) Any Unitarian we catch we lay out flat, or,
if he's left on his feet, we comrades – all Mazorca
men, of course – tie him from behind, and there
he stands, bound with a double hobble, elbows
knotted together, and above all stripped bare.
Savage! Here his ordeal begins.

[(22–33) Next, round his feet three loops of rawhide hold him tight, and he's straight as a picket,
prettily trussed. We keep him begging; we jab
at him, toying, and as he cries out we sing the

Slippery Dance and *snick-snick* without playing the violin.

[(34–51) But we keep rattling the brass sheaths that hold our knives and with our fingernails size up his throat. The cowardly savage starts, which makes us laugh! When some still in shirts collapse in tears, that's what most amuses us; our Chief likes it too and snorts with glee to hear the strains of music and the little joke we play on our trussed-up Unitarian.

[(52–63) After our larking about, when it suits us, we decide to cut the savage's breath. Straightaway one of us grabs a hank of his hair, while another pins him by the legs like a colt. Now, if he can move at all, it's only on all fours.

[(64–78) Meanwhile, he cries out to every saint in heaven; but there's no solace for his snivelling. Just below the ear, with a knife we call the pain-killer, whose blade is hard and sharp, we slit the veins of his neck. What happens next? He spurts blood, which is a pleasure, and in terror begins to roll his eyes.

[(79–87) Oh, the weakness of men! We've seen

some of these savages bite themselves, grimacing and making faces, their long tongues lolling; and between you and me there's no shame in giving one a kiss as a bit of gratification.

[(88–105) What a romp! We laugh and laugh to see them shudder; we next untie and set one savage loose, keeping him upright and watching him skate in his own blood – until he falls in a spasm, shaking and wildly kicking, then gradually goes still. When he lies dead, we flay a strip of his flesh that we can work to make a hobble.

[(106–11) Afterwards we lop his ears and beard, side-whiskers and brows; thus plucked he's flung aside to glut some bird of prey or pig.

[(112–15) So now you see, great Savage; nothing will befall you once we make you shout, 'Hurrah for the Federation!']

7
From 'Avellaneda'
by Esteban Echeverría

The following lines are from the close of Echeverría's long narrative poem 'Avellaneda', completed in Montevideo, in September 1849, and published there the next year. The excerpts below – Canto Three, Part VI, lines 159–95 and 206–32 – are reprinted from Vol. I of the poet's *Obras completas*, Buenos Aires, 1870, pp. 426–9. These are the passages that Gutiérrez refers to in his 1871 foreword to 'The Slaughteryard' (see p. 99).

      La señal dá un clarin, y estrepitosa
160   La música á tocar la *resvalosa*
      Empieza de repente,
      Y entre la chusma aquella el regocijo
      Circula como eléctrica corriente.
      Al oir la señal, cinco sayones
      Sobre las tristes víctimas se lanzan
      Y las tienden de espaldas á empellones;

Y mientras ellas roncan y patean
O en convulsiva lucha forcejean,
En su pecho clavando una rodilla
170   Y asiendo con la izquierda su cabello,
Al compás de la horrible resvalosa
Les hunden el cuchillo por el cuello.
Se oyen ayes y gritos sofocados
Y hervidero de sangre á borbollones,
Y de pies á cabeza ensangrentados
Se enderezan altivos los sayones.

Todo entonce es silencio;
De horror sobrecojida
Parece aquella turba, acostumbrada
180   Al crimen y á la sangre como al yugo
Del que es á un tiempo mismo
Su tirano emplacable y su verdugo,
Y en el dolor humano su deleite
Encuentra como un jénio del abismo.
Empero, de pié queda
Viendo ante sí los troncos palpitantes
De sus amigos degollados antes,
De horror estupefacto, Avellaneda:
Su verdugo feroz, en el delirio
190   Brutal de la venganza, calculando
Lo mas fino en crueldad, lo mas nefando
Para hacer mas acerbo su martirio,

Prolongarlo ha querido, y su alma impía
Deleitar observando
Del mártir el dolor y la agonía.

.   .   .   .

   Pero llega para él la hora postrera.
Vuelve á tocar la música sonora
La sonata agorera
De regocijo y de la matanza fiera,
210   Y un sayon se aproxima, y en la diestra
Resplandeciente daga
Sonriendo al mártir de la Patria muestra;
Su noble cuello con el filo amaga
Varias veces; lo hiere y sangre fluye. . . . .
Y se hiergue indignado, y arrojando
Mirada que electriza el torpe bando,
Exclama el mártir: – «Bárbaro, concluye;
No mas me martirices» – Fiero entonces
El sayon de estatura jigantesca
220   Lo tiende boca arriba; del cabello
Lo agarra, comprimiendo con la planta
Su pecho varoníl, y en un momento
A cuchillo cercena su garganta,
Como rebana el árbol de un achazo
Del montaraz el formidable brazo.
Un ay! resuena de profunda angustia,

Un áspero ronquido, y un murmullo,
Y el sayon levantando, ébrio de orgullo,
Muestra á la turva de terror transida
230   En la sangrienta mano suspendida,
Radiante de prestijio y de grandeza,
Del mártir de la Patria la cabeza.

[(159–76) A clarion gives the signal, all at once the noisy strains of the *resvalosa* start up, and glee runs through the mob like an electric current. Hearing the signal, five executioners hurl themselves on the unfortunate victims, throwing them down on their backs; and while the latter cry out, kick, and struggle frantically, a knee pins their chests, their hair is seized, and to the accompaniment of the hideous *resvalosa* a knife is sunk into their necks. Moaning, suffocated cries, throats gurgling and spurting blood; bathed in gore from head to toe, the arrogant killers get to their feet.

[(177–95) Then silence falls; the crowd is horror-struck, even though they are as used to crime and bloodshed as to the yoke of he who is at once their implacable tyrant, their scourge, and who – like some fiend from the abyss – revels in human suffering. But Avellaneda stands there, stunned with terror at the sight of the quivering bodies of his beheaded friends. His ruthless executioner, in the brutal madness of revenge, chooses to heighten and prolong the suffering by means of the most refined and evil cruelty, and his godless soul takes delight in watching the martyr's pain and agony.

[(206–32) But now the final hour has come. Once more the loud music plays the sonata that promises glee and a savage slaughter. The executioner approaches, glinting knife in hand; leering at our Country's martyr, he several times threatens the noble throat. At last, he wounds him, and blood flows. Bristling in anger, the martyr casts a glance that electrifies his clumsy opponent, and he calls out, 'Finish it, you savage, and end this torment.' Fierce then, the strapping executioner lays him out face up, gripping him by the hair and placing a foot on his manly chest; a moment later the knife slices into his throat the way a strong-armed woodsman's axe cuts into a tree. A groan of pain, a death rattle, a murmur; and the executioner, standing straight, drunk with glory and glowing with importance and pride, shows the terror-stricken crowd – hanging from his upraised, dripping hand – the head of our Country's martyr.]

Two of Echeverría's notes to Canto Three are also worth quoting. The first, number 6, appears on p. 443 of Vol. I of the *Obras completas*; the second, number 9, on p. 444.

6. Let us give a small example of the Federalist burlesque style made fashionable among his followers by Rosas, restorer of the art of writing as well as of the laws. The *Resvalosa* is a sonata of throat-cutting, and, as the word itself indicates, it enacts the sliding movement of a knife blade across a victim's throat and is sung and danced at the same time. The inventiveness of Rosas and the Federalists in bringing to perfection the arts of throat-cutting and theft cannot be denied.

The *mas-horca* [more gibbets] is a band of assassins, thieves, and throat-slitters founded and captained by Rosas the restorer of the laws himself. The group was formed with the above all-too-meaningful name. The *Resvalosa* is its own invention.

9. *Marco María Avellaneda* was decapitated in Metán on 3 October 1841, at the age of twenty-seven, on the orders of Oribe, and his head was stuck on a lance in the main square of Tucumán. His flayed body was quartered and hung from trees by the encampment at Metán. Oribe had the

skin made into switches and a lash, which he sent as a gift to Rosas. Any townspeople crossing the square, where the martyr's head was displayed, had to stop and look at it. Those who neglected or refused to comply with this order were set upon by the soldiers standing guard and whipped with the switches fashioned from Avellaneda's skin. 'This is your governor's hide,' the troops called out amid raucous laughter.

ENVOI

To Francis Spencer
and to Argentines everywhere

The hero of 'The Slaughteryard' is a young man. The heroes and martyrs of the struggle against Rosas were young men. In 1837, the annus mirabilis of Argentine history and letters, Echeverría was thirty-two years old; Juan Bautista Alberdi, twenty-seven; Juan María Guttiérrez, twenty-eight; Domingo Faustino Sarmiento, twenty-six; Marcos Sastre, twenty-eight; Hilario Ascasubi, thirty. Marco María Avellaneda was twenty-seven when he was decapitated and his head displayed in the main square of Tucumán. Rosas, in 1837, was forty-four.

The theme of youth and the hope of regeneration that youth implies run like a thread, a motif, an entreaty throughout Echeverría's prose. Into the throats of the fallen in the war of independence, he puts this cry: 'Rise up, rise up, Argentine patriots; rally round, young children of the fathers of our country. Let our hopes not be mocked' (*Dogma socialista*, 'A la juventud argentina', 21). Time and again he addresses and exhorts 'the new Generation' and 'the generations that will come'. And everywhere, even in the darkest hours, his message burns with the bright lamp of hope.

My own relationship with Argentina goes back to the dark days of 1968 and the military dictatorship of General Onganía, when, as I recorded, 'grim-faced Federal police, more of them every week, appeared on the street corners wearing jackboots and nasty submachine guns.' With the regularity of a clock, one military dictator supplanted another. Worse, far worse, was to come. I had many friends in Buenos Aires; I loved them and, despite the threatening gloom, I had grown to love the place. But when a son was born there in 1971 my fears for his safety won out over my sentimental allegiances and I left Buenos Aires for Britain. From there I observed the cancer spreading and spreading. In 1976, no less a figure than Borges emerged from the Casa Rosada – Argentina's seat of government – to inform the world that the coup-led command, now under General Jorge Videla, was in the hands of gentlemen. I was aghast. Videla had usurped power and was set to unleash a regime of state terrorism that far outstripped anything perpetrated by Rosas. My personal lamp of hope guttered out.

But it didn't for others. There were brave souls who refused to give up or give in. One was the writer and journalist Andrew Graham-Yooll, who daily risked his neck at the *Buenos Aires Herald* recording and publishing the names of the civilians whom the gentlemen who ruled the country were abducting, torturing, and executing without trial. Finally, like so many Argentines before him, Andrew had to seek safety abroad for himself and his family. Thanks to Amnesty International and the French government, Air France flew him from the River Plate and he took up residence in London. In Andrew, the lamp of hope never flickered, never deserted him. He was, perhaps all unknowing, a true son and follower of Echeverría. Andrew penned one of the grimmest and truest books ever written about the Argentine, *In a State of Fear*, a work that is a rare masterpiece. Graham-Yooll was thirty-two when he embarked on his exile; it lasted for eighteen years.

I know that this book, *The Slaughteryard*, presents a harsh, black, damning view of Argentine society. I know that warnings about history – no matter how salutary their intention – make for painful reading. I only wish it could be otherwise.

Of course I feel solidarity with thinking Argentines and to them I wish only to extend encouragement. Echeverría and his companions are still sublime examples of Argentine patriots who dared think for themselves. Their spirit and idealism still embody hope – hope for common decency, for the rule of law, for democratic institutions, for justice. This is what Echeverría and his *Dogma socialista* have to offer the young of Argentina today – solace, comfort, and wisdom not only for their native land but for all humanity.

Reading and re-reading Echeverría gives us a sense of innocent individuals in their thousands crowding round with unvoiced voices – Argentines of Rosas' time and since – desperate for recognition and redress, desperate to be heard. To all such victims we have a debt of honour, just as we have a debt of honour everywhere and in every age to victims of social injustice.

N.T. di G.

Acknowledgements

The translation and preparation of this book were mainly a job of reading and study. Fundamental, then, was access to materials held by the British Library, the London Library, and the University of Southampton's Hartley Library. I am particularly grateful to the British Library's Dr Barry Taylor, Curator of Hispanic Collections, 1501–1850, and to Dr Geoffrey West, Head of the Hispanic Section.

Argentine state institutions, as well as suffering from political vagaries, pillage, and underfunding, are a bureaucratic nightmare. One therefore shuns them. Unless – as with much else in Buenos Aires – you are lucky enough to have a patron. I did, which smoothed the way at the Argentine National Library and made my sojourn there painless. For this, I am indebted to Josefina Delgado, the library's former Deputy Director. My thanks also to Noemí Cavallo, head of the library's rare book room, the Sala del Tesoro.*

---

* Argentines will bridle at what I have written here, but the details of a fuller story are even worse. Five or so years

Acknowledgements

Coming from the outside world and adapting to a fiercely individualistic Argentina, the researcher looks for help not from public institutions but from fellow enthusiasts, private collectors, private libraries, and, most beneficently, from antiquarian booksellers. Often it is unnecessary even to look; Argentine generosity is such that help frequently appears out of thin air. Among the antiquarians, I am especially grateful to Víctor Aizenman, Gustavo Breitfeld, Alberto Casares, and Washington Pereyra for their good will and practical advice. Pereyra, also founder and president of the Fundación Bartolomé Hidalgo, a homely museum-library-research centre for literary sleuths – located out in the hinterland (but

---

ago, it was reported in the local press that the then director of the institution found that of its 334 employees only four were trained in librarianship and that a considerable number of them were stealing and selling the library's books. When he began to lock away certain valuable items, the staff hassled him, thereby prompting his resignation. Even during Borges's administration, when the Biblioteca Nacional was at its old address in Calle México, there was a scandal involving the theft and sale of incunabula by the library's employees. Borges's gnomic response to this clandestine activity was that nobody can actually own a book. Years earlier in one of his essays he had lamented that 'the Argentine is an individual, not a citizen' and that 'to him, stealing public funds is not a crime.' So much for civic enlightenment in the Argentine Republic.

really the geographical heart) of Buenos Aires –
gave me free access to his holdings.

At some point, my investigations led me to the
Furt library. The collection, a little-known jewel,
is housed in the buildings of an early estancia,
Los Talas, near Luján, some seventy miles west of
Buenos Aires. This was the estancia that belonged
to Echeverría's brother. I was accompanied there
by María Adelina Abraham and Carlos Dámaso
Martínez, himself an Echeverría expert and com-
piler of an edition of 'El matadero'. We arrived
without an appointment on a day when the
premises were closed to visitors. But when I said I
had travelled from England, we were immediately
led to an inner sanctum where in semi-darkness
I could leaf through an incomparable shelf of
Echeverría first editions. We were also shown the
small room where Echeverría wrote some of his
poems and may even have penned 'El matadero'.

My thanks also to the following: Susan Ashe
for her collaboration and infinite patience in the
unravelling of Echeverría and Gutiérrez's texts
and the making of these English versions; Francis
Spencer and René de Costa, early readers of the
English version, for criticism; Marcial Souto, for
every kind of help and encouragement and, in
particular, for his patience in dealing with my

typographical demands; the poet Hugo Ditaranto for providing valuable historical insights, for confirming various hunches of my own, and for his poem, which follows these notes; Fernando Burgos, who gave me a copy of his critical edition of 'El matadero', which was endlessly useful; Leonor Fleming, whose excellent edition of Echeverría's text started me on my journey and who allowed me to pick her brains along the way; Félix Weinberg for the gift of his bibliography of Echeverría; and Vanessa Jouning for certain early typographical orientation.

I have also benefitted from the encouragement and suggestions of two Argentine scholars, Luis Chitarroni and Roberto Yahni.

I am grateful as well to John Glad, who tracked down and sent me copies of two earlier English translations of Echeverría's story – those by Angel Flores (1959) and by John Incledon (1983), titled, respectively, *The Slaughter House* and 'The Slaughterhouse'; and to José Luis Goyena, who found me one in French, *L'Abattoir*, by Paul Verdevoye (1997).

David Hayden, Susan Ashe, Michele McKay Aynesworth, Francis Spencer, Jason Wilson, Marcial Souto, and my son Tom di Giovanni were helpful in their critical reading of my introduction.

Acknowledgements

My son Derek di Giovanni has provided firm support by teaching me to use my website as a kind of palimpsest.

Thanks to Liz Cowen for a final meticulous reading of the whole book.

Albert Palco's magisterial edition of Echeverría's *Dogma socialista*, bringing together a wealth of material, has been indispensable. As has been Pedro Orgambide and Roberto Yahni's *Enciclopedia de la literatura argentina*. The former dates from 1940; the latter from 1970.

I leave for last acknowledgement of the debt I owe to one particular book, which was a source of great inspiration to me at the outset of my ransacking of printed work about Echeverría and his times. That volume is José Luis Lanuza's beautifully conceived and beautifully written *Esteban Echeverría y sus amigos*, first published in Buenos Aires in 1951, the centenary of Echeverría's death.

That the issues of Echeverría's story – stifling autocracy, bullying and cruelty, ruthless repression and blind allegiance to fanaticism – had currency until recently not only in the Argentine but throughout Latin America will not be news to any student of current affairs. To Argentines who know their history and who have the capacity to think, the Rosas period remains a living nightmare. One contemporary writer's struggle with the long reverberation of his country's past can be glimpsed in the following lines, written in 1994 or 1995 and given here in an English approximation:

Throat-cutting
by Hugo Ditaranto

Beyond a calling, a vice,
a way of life.
Despicable, insane,
it was an incinerated book,
a throatless cry,
space without air,
the random bullet that strikes the heart.
Ours is a past of blunted knives,
a time of grief.
Our history is terror,
is rape.

ESTEBAN ECHEVERRÍA, born in Buenos Aires, 2 September 1805; died in Montevideo, 19 January 1851. His *Obras completas*, edited by his friend and biographer Juan María Gutiérrez, were published in Buenos Aires, in five volumes, 1870–74.

NORMAN THOMAS DI GIOVANNI's association with Argentina goes back forty or more years, when Jorge Luis Borges invited him to Buenos Aires. He has translated work by at least fifty different Argentine writers – including twelve books by Borges, all of which have been proscribed and are currently rumoured to be appearing in samizdat editions – and has also, with Susan Ashe, edited and translated two anthologies of Argentine short stories, *Celeste Goes Dancing*, in 1989, and *Hand in Hand Alongside the Tracks*, in 1992. Born in New England, di Giovanni has been a naturalized European citizen since 1992 and now lives in England. In 1991, the Argentine government appointed him a Commander of the Order of May. A new edition of his memoir and essays on Borges, *The Lesson of the Master*, will appear in the Library of Lost Books in the autumn of 2010.

SUSAN ASHE was born in northern India, and in 1947 moved to England. She is the author of *Cuda of the Celts* (2003) and *Fillet and the Mob* (2004) and has also produced a number of literary translations from the French, Spanish, and Italian.